Author Praise for *Clearing Customs*

"Has Carl Hiaasen switched states and gender or what???
Is the best-selling mystery novelist now targeting his noir
satires not at Florida but New Mexico, going undercover
as a Santa Fe gallery owner named Martha Egan? Egan's
Clearing Customs wages jihad on the same brand of
self-serving cretins that overpopulate Hiaasen's Miami,
heavy-handed, power hungry, sloppy politicos and so-called
public servants too ready to break the law to enforce it.
And anybody who loves Hiaasen will have a ball reading Egan's
fast-paced, chili-flavored, and always entertaining mystery."

BOB SHACOCHIS
American Book Award, 1985, *Easy in the Islands;*
Prix de Rome, 1989, *The Next New World*

"Thanks to Martha Egan for giving us Beverly—a river
running, shop-keeping protagonist who doesn't look like a
Barbie doll—to propel her page turning story about a brave new
world where privacy does not exist. Read this book at your
own risk. You may never feel the same about your mail,
your phone, or your life."

ELIZABETH COHEN
author of *The Family on Beartown Road,*
a *New York Times* Notable Book, 2003

"In *Clearing Customs,* Martha Egan has written a flaming
indictment of government bureaucracy run amok."

JACK LOEFFLER
author of *Adventures with Ed: A Portrait of Abbey*

"Can a novel about a 42-year-old ex-hippie who describes herself as 'built like a Buick' and her entanglement with the U.S. Customs Service become a grip? The answer is, yes! With clarity, honesty, humor, and emotional depth, *(Clearing Customs)* draws the reader into a narrative that rings with authenticity, a tale about the absurd, insane games that out-of-control 'special agents' play with those they select as targets, citizens like you and me."

WICK DOWNING
author of *Leonardo's Hand*

"If you suspected the government was tapping your phone, following you around, and otherwise harassing you unjustly, you could passively ascribe it all to paranoia, or, like Beverly Parmentier, the protagonist in this exciting novel, you could fight back. . . . a terrific and engaging story."

FRED HARRIS
former US Senator, (D-OK),
author of *Following the Harvest*

"*Clearing Customs* . . . is a witty, smart and provocative take on the intrusions of the federal government into the lives of private citizens."

GEORGIA JONES-DAVIS
The Santa Fe New Mexican

"If revenge is a dish best eaten cold, Martha Egan has taken 16 years to freeze herself a vengeful Popsicle of a book."

PATRICIA MILLER
The Durango Herald

COYOTA

ALSO BY MARTHA EGAN

*   *   *   *   *

Clearing Customs
Relicarios: Devotional Miniatures of the Americas
Milagros: Votive Offerings from the Americas

COYOTA

* * * * *

A NOVEL

MARTHA EGAN

Papalote Press

Santa Fe

This is a work of fiction. Any resemblance to persons or incidents from the generally accepted collective hallucination that we loosely refer to as "reality" is purely coincidental and not to be taken seriously.

Grateful acknowledgement is made to the Museum of New Mexico Press for permission to quote from *A Dictionary of New Mexico and Southern Colorado Spanish* by Rubén Cobos. Copyright 1983.

Papalote Press
P.O. Box 32058
Santa Fe, NM 87594
www.papalotepress.com

ISBN 978-0-975588-12-3 cloth
ISBN 978-0-975588-13-0 paper
Library of Congress Control Number 2004107829

FIRST PRINTING
This book is printed on acid-free, archival-quality paper.
Manufactured in the USA.

9   8   7   6   5   4   3   2   1

coyote,-ta, *m.* and *f.* [<Mex. Sp. *coyote*] said of the youngest child in a family; offspring of a mixed Anglo-American Indo-Hispanic marriage; native, of the country . . .

RUBÉN COBOS
A Dictionary of New Mexico and
Southern Colorado Spanish

PROLOGUE

There was a bridge. Narrow. Narrower than the anemic, winding road that led down to it from the slopes on either side of the canyon, a deep gash knifing through dry hills that on this moonless night were mottled with the shadowy forms of boulders and cacti, an army of silent desert sentinels. The bridge was old, cobbled out of crumbling gray cement and volcanic rock the color of dried blood. Its pavement was cracked and pebbly with wear and neglect. Gleaming glass shards littered the roadbed and the edges of the cliff, mirroring millions of stars that glittered overhead in a bottomless black sky.

The tiny night sounds of scurrying rodents and the predators that hunt them were suddenly obscured by the rumble of two cars approaching the bridge from the south. One produced a thin, strained whine. The other a more powerful noise, low and angry. With a resounding roar the larger vehicle gained ground on the smaller one and drew alongside it as they both neared the precipice. There was a pause, followed by a volley of explosions, metal and glass blasting through the chasm, the sound screaming up the mountainsides, rocking boulders loose, shaking cacti to their roots, startling sleep-drugged birds into shaky flight. In a cacophony of destruction, metal and rock clashed against each other time and again, as one of the vehicles bounded and tumbled into the barranca's depths, pursued by a shower of loosened stones and fractured glass, until at last it rocked to a halt in the dry stream bed hundreds of feet below the bridge. A cloud of dust and smoke billowed out of the gorge, veiling the faint blue starlight.

A low animal sound, eerie and unearthly, feeble at first, gathered strength and rebounded through the canyon, in whose depths, where the vehicle lay crumpled and steaming, a light wind swirled like the stir of batwings. A rustle in the clumps of dried grass that lined the arroyo. A humid gust of breath, a wind whisper that shuddered up the canyon walls through the brush, ruffling the fur of tiny frightened animals crouched in its shadows. Higher and higher it rose, up over the bridge, over the mountains into the black void beyond.

Then the creak and ping of cooling metal in the ravine's depths, the whoo of a lone owl, and the light retreating step of a coyote that had watched it all from a craggy overhang.

1

Like a drowning woman struggling toward the ocean surface, Nena Herrera-Casey willed herself awake from a bizarre, terrifying dream. Fear clutched her like a huge, cold hand. Her heart beat wildly. Her legs quivered and ached. Although she felt raw and hollow, she clenched her eyes shut and groped her way back into her slumber to piece the dream together again. If she could recall it, if she could make sense of it, she might be able to conquer its terror. Through the fog of sleep, parts of the dream slowly reappeared. A craggy, desert hillside, cacti standing like sentries in a black night, an old bridge, violent explosions. She saw a vehicle careen off the bridge and plunge into the deep arroyo beneath it. Was she in that car? Was it anyone she knew? The setting was not familiar, but Nena did remember a coyote trotting away in the dark. A gray ghost slipping through cactus.

Like an ebbing tide, the nightmare rapidly receded into her subconscious. Nena stretched toward the shore of wakefulness. As she blinked her eyes to clear them, the *latilla* ceiling of her bedroom changed from a striped blur to neat rows of split cedar in the dawn light. She tossed back the covers, swung her still-aching legs over the side of the mattress, and planted her feet on the Zapotec rug beside her bed. She rose slowly, shaking her head as if to dislodge the remnants of the disturbing dream from her consciousness. Her long, straight, shiny hair cascaded around the almond oval of her face like curtains of blue-black silk.

She dressed in her winter jogging gear and stepped out of her small adobe farmhouse for an early morning run. "Maybe a good workout will defuse the nightmare," she thought as she jogged down the packed earth trail that paralleled the irrigation ditch near her house.

The blue December sky was still pale. Her breath left frosty puffs in her wake as she lengthened her stride and pushed herself a little faster, her heart drumming in time to her footfalls. Beyond the landscape of scattered houses and small farms to the east, a gilded sphere was rising above the Sandía Mountains, promising a clear, sunny day. The ditchbank ran ahead for miles, until it disappeared into the *bosque,* the dry tangle of trees, red willow, and brush along the Río Grande. In spring, this *acequia* would be brimming, transporting water from the river to the Corrales Valley's parched fields and orchards. Now, in the middle of an unusually cold winter, it was dry and empty, serving only to ensnare vagrant tumbleweeds and trash.

At this hour, Nena had the landscape to herself. Only now and then a car or truck appeared, raising clouds of dust on the unpaved roads. As she jogged past a grove of skeletal cottonwoods, a coven of ravens cawed loudly to each other, bouncing up and down on the trees' bare branches before flapping off into the translucent gold sky. On the far side of the river, Albuquerque's early morning traffic roared like a distant waterfall.

A mile and a half down the ditch, Nena reached her turn-around point, where a paved road passed over a culvert. Abruptly, a coyote sped out of the acequia, vaulted the path in front of her in a blur of brown and gray, and dove into the chaparral. There he stopped, spun around, and studied her with slanted yellow eyes.

Nena had to smile. "Scared you, didn't I, Señor Coyote!" She laughed. Nonplussed, the coyote trotted away, his colors blending easily with the sand sage and chamisa.

She was thrilled to encounter coyotes on her morning jogs. Although Corrales was becoming a bedroom community for Albuquerque, coyotes, as well as rabbits, quail, road runners, bobcats, and other wildlife still made their home in the valley's hidden places.

When she was a little girl, coyotes frightened her. Her Apache grandmother, Libertad, cured her of that notion. "They're God's dogs, *m'hija*," she said. "Very special animals. Strong, quick, wise, and clever enough to get themselves out of danger. And they'll never hurt you. Don't fear them—be like them. They're survivors."

Nena developed a strong affinity for coyotes. She repeatedly drew them for school art projects, she cut pictures of them out of magazines, she even tried to imitate their howls and yips. Her older brother Luis began to call her *Coyota,* and so did the whole family. They still fascinated her. Now, nearly every night, as she drifted off to sleep, she felt comforted listening to the coyotes sing their undulating choruses to the moon.

*   *   *   *   *

The jog home was always quicker, and soon, she trotted onto a narrow trail that led to her street, a potholed dirt track the locals grandly called Casey Boulevard. At the end of her driveway, she slowed to a walk and stooped to retrieve *The Albuquerque Journal* from its customary landing spot in a clump of currant bushes. Trailing plumes of steamy breath, she opened her back door.

The kitchen clock showed eight. She was nearly half an hour behind schedule, with barely enough time for a quick shower before heading out the door to her appointment with U.S. Customs at nine. Maybe the nightmare that caused her to oversleep and feel sluggish had made her run slower than usual. Breakfast was going to be what she called a "Toyota Special": a cold flour tortilla slapped with butter and jam, washed down with a bottle of orange juice as she drove her truck to the airport.

She kicked off her running shoes and headed for the shower.

2

Nena reached the old airport parking lot with several minutes to spare. As she swung a large cloth messenger bag over her shoulder and locked her truck, she heard a voice behind her.

"*¡Profesora!*"

A young man in faded jeans and a denim jacket approached her smiling. He seemed familiar, but she couldn't place him.

"*¡Soy Carlos!* Your Spanish 101 class two years ago."

Now Nena remembered him and took his outstretched hand. "*¿Cómo estás, Carlos?*"

"*¡Fantástico!*" he replied. "*Voy a casar mi amor in El Paso.*"

"Congratulations!" Nena said. "You're getting married?"

"Yup," he said. "This weekend. Oops—I forget how to say *weekend* in Spanish."

"*Fin de semana,*" Nena said. "*Me caso este fin de semana.*"

"You, too? You're getting married this weekend *también?* What an amazing coincidence!" He laughed.

Nena laughed, too. Carlos was the class clown, always making jokes and teasing. Slightly older than the others, he knew tidbits of street Spanish and was sometimes cocky about it. Still he was likeable, a quick learner who enlivened the class with his banter.

"Are you still a *piloto?*" she asked.

"*Si, profesora. Soy piloto privado con mi propria compañía de aviación.*"

Nena laughed. She had worked with him on that phrase:

"I'm a private pilot with my own aviation company." Carlos was proud of being a pilot, a profession that set him apart from the younger students. He said he flew to Mexico often, transporting electronic equipment and engine parts.

"Hey, you haven't forgotten! I'm pleased you're keeping up with your Spanish. And congratulations on your wedding. I'd love to hear more about what you've been up to, but I've got to run. Please excuse me. I need to be at customs in two minutes. *¡Adiós!*" Nena called as she waved goodbye.

*   *   *   *   *

She pushed open the metal door to the building where customs and a brokerage firm had their offices. A heavy-set, balding customs inspector looked up from behind a jumble of cardboard boxes piled on a long metal counter. "*Qué suerte,*" she said to herself, pleased to see that Clark Bisbee would be clearing her shipment. He was the nicest and most reasonable of the three Albuquerque inspectors.

Bisbee smiled at Nena and glanced at his watch. "Right on the button. Good girl! But I'm afraid I have bad news for you," he said, nodding toward a pile of brown and white wool sweaters heaped on the counter.

Nena groaned. "No invoices?"

"No, they included invoices, and the paperwork actually seems to match up with the shipment for a change. Your friends in Ecuador forgot to label the sweaters."

She glumly set down her bag. "That damn co-op. I've been working with them for over a decade and they still can't get it right. However, being an old Girl Scout, I came prepared. I brought some with me."

She smiled at the inspector hopefully. She knew it was within his power to confiscate and destroy the entire shipment because of the exporter's lapse, which would mean a loss of more than a thousand dollars for her. Bisbee was usually fair, unlike certain other inspectors she had dealt with. If she were lucky, he would allow her to sew in tags, re-inspect the shipment, and release it to her.

She took a small white cotton rectangle out of her bag and gave it to him.

He read it out loud. "'100% wool, Cooperativa Imbabura, Handmade in Ecuador, Dry Clean Only.' Looks fine to me, Nena. Make sure you sew them down on all four corners."

"If you don't mind, I'll work on them now. My Spanish 101 class isn't until one."

"That's fine. What are you doing in a beginning Spanish class, if I may ask, Ms. Herrera-Casey?"

"I'm teaching it. I'm a part-time instructor at UNM, a couple of Spanish classes. It's a sideline to my regular job of sewing labels into unmarked imports."

Bisbee laughed. "This is going to take you a while, you know. There are forty sweaters here. Call me when you're through. I'll be in the office." He opened a frosted-glass-paned door lettered U.S. CUSTOMS SERVICE and disappeared inside.

Nena took out her needle and thread and a small bag of the handmade labels she made the last time the coop sent her a shipment of unmarked woolens. She sat cross-legged on the grimy metal counter next to the heap of sweaters, and began to stitch. For over three hours she worked in the drafty customs clearing area, methodically tacking the four corners of each rectangle into the neck of each bulky *chompa*. Forty sweaters. One hundred sixty corners. Yards and yards of thread, bitten off into two-foot-lengths, enough for two sweaters. Aching wrists, a sore cold bottom. Numerous pinpricks in her numbed fingertips. With every stitch she regretted never learning to use a thimble. She tried to think about her upcoming class and drills she could do with her students, who were struggling with *ser* and *estar,* the two verb forms in Spanish for "to be." But she was increasingly uncomfortable and cranky as she worked on the sweaters as quickly as possible.

"Stupid, pointless rules. Stupid, ugly labels. Stupid needle with the impossibly small eye!" She muttered to herself. "Why doesn't one of the customs guys at least offer me a chair or maybe a nice hot cup of coffee?"

Noises coming from inside the customs office a few feet from where she sat provided a background to her soundless mechanical chore: the shrill ring of phones, the opening and closing screech of metal file cabinets, the clack of computer printers, the beep of faxes, and the murmur of conversations. Nena gradually became aware of two deep male voices talking in undertones on the other side of a closed door behind her.

". . . big celebration . . ."

". . . drink lunch with him."

"El Paso . . ."

"When he goes to drain his lizard, we fix his tanks . . ."

" . . . any minute now—kaboom!"

There was laughter.

"Chuckie's last drop . . ."

More laughter.

" . . . inhaled his last rail . . ."

" . . . kicked his last bale . . ."

" . . . told his last tale . . ."

The conversation gradually sifted into her mind. "What are they talking about?" She hesitated in mid-stitch to pay closer attention. Inside the office, a door slammed with a rattle of window glass. Suddenly the men stopped talking. Nena heard Inspector Bisbee's voice. "You Drug Enforcement dudes sure seem to have a lot of time on your hands."

The men sniggered.

Bisbee spoke again. "She still out there?"

"Who?" both men asked in unison.

Nena heard someone walking her way and hurriedly finished her last stitch. The door opened, and Inspector Bisbee stepped into the hall, a sheaf of papers in hand. Behind him, Nena saw two men start as they caught sight of her. One was short and stocky, with glasses, thinning blond hair, and a grease-stained orange jumpsuit. He gazed at her in open-mouthed wonder. The other was taller and heavy-set, with dark frizzy hair, and an air of undisguised hostility. A jagged scar ran down his cheek from the corner of his right eye, disappearing into his trim, salt and pepper beard. His puffy, hairy hands gripped the lapels of a black leather jacket that hung open over a snap-fastened western shirt and tight black jeans.

Inspector Bisbee closed the door behind him. The glass clattered. "Got 'em done, Nena?"

"Your timing is perfect. This is the last one," she said, tying a knot in the thread, biting it off, and tossing the sweater onto a thick woolly heap of its siblings. She stuck the needle into the spool of thread and dropped it into her bag.

"Good job," he said, barely glancing at the sweaters. He set the paperwork down on top of a carton, signed several pages with a flourish, and handed them to her. "The duties come to two hundred eighty-three seventy-two," he announced.

She wrote out a check to the U.S. Customs Service and gave it to him. With a wave of his hand, he disappeared into his office.

Nena scooped up her sweaters and dumped them into their battered boxes that seemed to be held together solely by sundry shipping tags and strips of yellow U.S. Customs tape. She loaded the cartons onto a dolly, rolled them out the rear door to the loading dock, and went to fetch her truck.

As she was pushing the last box into her Toyota, she noticed the short man in the orange jumpsuit standing at the low chain-link fence that bordered the tarmac alongside the old airport building. He smoked a cigarette as he gazed absently at the main Albuquerque airport terminal, his free hand jammed into the chest pocket of his soiled overalls. Then he faced her, his lips tightened into a self-satisfied sneer. His hostile expression sent ice water rippling down her spine. Defiantly, she stared back and memorized his face: the stubby nose, the black-rimmed glasses, the faintly pock-marked skin, the furry eyebrows that nearly met beneath an overhang of dirty blond hair.

He took a last drag on his cigarette and flipped the still-burning butt into the bushes. With ease, he vaulted the four-foot-high wire fence, his airport identity badge flapping, and quickly strode southwest across the tarmac where his buddy in the leather jacket was waiting in a small tanker truck. They sped off toward the general aviation ramp, where dozens of small planes were parked.

A sense of unease washed over Nena. "Creepy guys," she thought as she watched the men leave. She closed up her camper shell and drove to the University of New Mexico.

3

The next morning, as Nena opened the back door after her run, she heard the telephone's insistent ring from the kitchen. She tossed the morning paper onto the washing machine and went to answer it. "Must be Mamá calling," she decided. "No one else would dare phone me before eight a.m. and let it ring fifteen times." She picked up the receiver.

"María Azucena—," a voice said.

Nena was right. It was her mother, addressing her by her formal name. Only she and her relatives, the Mexican side of the family, called her that. "Hi, *Mamita. Buenos días te dé Dios.* How are you?"

"Ay, *m'hijita,* not so good. This arturitis give me terrible pains. Is killing me slowly. Nothing helps. *Nada.* Last night I don't sleep five minutes."

"I'm sorry, Mamita. I'm working on putting together an old-fashioned New Mexican *remedio* for you, the one Grandmother Libertad used to give people for arthritis. She said it really works."

"Eee, your *abuela, esa india.* I guess you mean that *mota* and alcohol thing? Please don't, *hija!* That's all I need. My unmarry daughter get arrest for marijuana. Then the university never give you a real job. Nobody give you a real job."

"The university is probably never going to give me a real job anyway, Mom. I keep telling you that," Nena said, rolling her eyes in exasperation. "When they can hire TA's like me to teach for eight dollars an hour part-time with no benefits, why should they ever offer me anything better?"

"You have all those degrees, m'hija," her mother clucked. "You could get a respectable job with them. Maybe your sister can help you get hire at the bank. Make your mother proud."

Nena began to smolder. She took a deep breath, gritted her teeth, and flashed the telephone a cheesy smile. "I am doing just fine, Mother," she said with feigned serenity. "I love my job at UNM, and I love my weekend flea market business. They're both real jobs to me. I probably make more money than Crucita does as a teller, and I have my freedom. I'm sorry if you don't approve. *Así es la vida*—that's life! But I'm going to be late for my 9:30 conversation class if I don't get off the phone."

"Just one more thing, María Azucena. I want invite that young man for Christmas dinner with us."

Nena knew exactly who her mother was referring to, but she couldn't help herself. "¡Ay, Mamita! You have a young man now? Is this anybody we know?"

"Do not make jokes, Azucena," her mother said peevishly. "Is your friend I want invite. I never betray your father's memory. I am marry with my Sebastián forever. Not matter how long he is gone. He is still with me. For always."

Nena sighed. This was an old argument. Since her father's death ten years ago, her mother had spurned numerous suitors. "If the young man you mean is my friend, Caldwell, Mother, I think he's leaving town over the holidays."

Nena didn't think Cal was going anywhere, but their relationship, such as it was, was definitely not ready for an Herrera-Casey family Christmas dinner, an event she'd once described as a food fight in a chimp cage. No matter that he expressed interest in meeting her family, said he wanted to learn Spanish, and claimed his own family gatherings were "boisterous affairs." She wouldn't soon subject Caldwell Oates Banner III to such an ordeal.

"I have to go, Mom. Really. Thanks for calling." She hung up the phone and raced into the bathroom for a quick shower. She truly was going to be late if she didn't hurry. Once again, breakfast was going to be a Toyota Special. Maybe Cal would be free for coffee after her class. By then she would be dying of caffeine withdrawal. Even the student union's dreadful watery coffee would fit the bill if he couldn't meet her in their usual spot at Café Olé across from the university.

On her way out the door, she picked up the newspaper and tucked it into a side pocket of her messenger bag. Maybe she could read it between classes.

4

From her cubbyhole office in the modern languages department, she made a quick call to Cal before heading off to class. "10:45 at our usual spot?" she asked when he answered.

"You're on," he said.

After class, as she waited under a swag of fluttering *papel picado* flags in the cheerfully decorated café, she took the newspaper out of her bag and unrolled it. A bold headline announced:

SMALL PLANE CRASHES

Albuquerque, December 17—Albuquerque International Airport officials reported the crash of a single-engine Cessna 210 at about 1 p.m. Wednesday. According to airport manager L.J. Harriman, eyewitnesses said that shortly after taking off to the southeast the small plane's engine sputtered and seemed to quit. As hundreds of passengers and airport workers watched, the plane corkscrewed into an arroyo south of the airport and burst into flames on impact. The pilot was killed instantly. Harriman said there were no passengers. The pilot's name has not yet been released, pending notification of next of kin. The National Transportation Safety Board and airport police are investigating the crash.

Stunned, Nena put down the newspaper. "Jesus! I left the airport at about 12:30, a mere half-hour before the crash," she realized, shuddering. "How awful! If I'd stayed longer, I might have seen it."

A hand on her shoulder startled Nena back to the present. She dropped the newspaper and smiled up at Cal. He set his tall glass of caffè latte down, sat beside her, and took a big slurp.

"You look like that milk ad," she laughed.

"Milk ad . . . ," he muttered, the brow under his mop of blond curls furrowed in concentration as he bent over his glass for another sip.

"Yeah, the one with celebrities like Spike Lee and Larry King wearing milk mustaches."

"On TV?" He frowned, the café's lights gleaming off his thick eyeglasses as he tipped his head back and peered at her.

"In the print media," she explained. "It's in all the mags—*People, Vanity Fair, George, Medieval Monthly . . .*"

Cal tore a napkin from the dispenser and swiped at his mouth. "Is it gone now?"

"Yes, it's gone. But it was cute."

"Cute?"

"Yeah, cute."

Cal Banner's frown dissolved into a wry smile. *"Medieval Monthly?"*

Nena grinned shyly. "Whatever it is you history profs read."

"I can only speak for myself. I seem to read a lot of very boring gobbledygook. The kind of stuff I'm supposed to have my grad students write. The kind of stuff *I'm* supposed to write, if I ever want to get tenure here. Ugh. I need a vacation."

"Me too," Nena said, resting her chin on the palm of her

hand as she smiled at him, taking in the way he arched his reddish whiskery eyebrows when he was thinking, his mouth a rosy pucker, his finger ready to push his rimless glasses back up the slippery slope of his ski-jump nose.

"Say," he said, plunking his glass down. "Do you have any holiday break plans?"

"I've been toying with the idea of a trip to Mexico."

"Mexico? That sounds so far away, so exotic."

"Not so far away. The border is only four hours from here. And it's not exotic to me. Don't forget I'm half-Mexican. My mother's family is from Dolores Hidalgo."

"Dolores . . . Oh, the movie star?" Cal grinned. "She was in *Madame DuBarry!*"

Nena laughed. "You are toooo silly! That was Dolores del Río. Dolores Hidalgo's a small city near Guanajuato. Sort of west central Mexico."

"Near Mexico City?"

"About five hours to the northwest. Guanajuato's an old mining town, the capital of the state of the same name. It's a colonial era gem. Maybe you've heard of the Cervantes Festival?"

"Of course! The Guarneri played there last year. Guano . . . How do you pronounce it?"

"Wahn-ah-whah-toh. Now say after me . . ."

"I will not."

"You told me you wanted to learn Spanish."

"I do. Of course I do! But not here. Not in front of God and everybody, Nena. Although I guess I do need to learn the lingo if I'm going to stay in New Mexico. In my very first class here last fall, I was reading out the names of the students and no one answered when I called out "Chaves"—as in 'rhymes with knaves.' I found out the hard way that the student's name was Chá-vez."

Nena burst into laughter.

Cal frowned. "That's exactly what the entire class did. They howled. I've never been so humiliated!" He leaned over and rested his forehead against Nena's, then gave her a discreet kiss before taking another sip of coffee. "Say, you wouldn't happen to know a good Spanish teacher who might be free for a week or two at the holidays, do you?"

∗   ∗   ∗   ∗   ∗

The weekend before, Nena's brother Luis had quizzed her about her new beau while he fixed her hot water heater. "So who is this dude you're seeing, Coyota?"

"Oh, he teaches medieval European history. It's his second year here. A French prof introduced us."

"And . . . ?" Luis grinned. "How come we haven't met him?"

"We've only been going out for a few months. You'll meet him one of these days—as long as you promise not to pounce on him."

"Pounce? Me? Your big bro'? Your confidant? C'mon, Nena, what's he like?"

"Well, he's a little formal, but he has a terrific sense of humor, and he cooks me fabulous dinners. I think he's from a fairly wealthy family in Newport. He went away to prep school, summer camps, vacations with his family in France—the usual Northeastern *rico* wasp thing."

"Uncle Lorenzo is having a *matanza* next week in Los Lunas. They're slaughtering two pigs. Think we should invite your friend?" Luis asked with a twinkle in his eye.

"Oh, God, he'd die!" Nena giggled.

She was a little defensive about Cal. He wasn't like Luis and the other men she grew up with—guys who knew how to fix a truck or build an adobe house, men who were physically strong, capable, macho. Cal dwelled in another world. He was a few years younger than Nena, courtly, and completely at home in the world of ideas, books, music, and art. He insisted on paying for their evenings out, and he gave her little gifts. But he wasn't a fix-it kind of guy. The previous week, his BMW had a flat tire, and he called AAA. Nena was going to offer to change it for him, but she stopped herself.

Of course, what she didn't tell her brother was that for the last month or so, she had spent several nice sexy evenings with Cal.

5

Strolling back to her office, Nena hummed a Mozart ditty of the sort Cal often played for her. Although the December day was chilly and a somber gray, she wasn't cold in the least. She felt positively tropical and sunny, in fact, considering the possibility of a trip to Mexico with him. It could be a lot of fun.

Josefa, the department's veteran secretary, met her in the hallway. "Have you seen this afternoon's *Trib*?" she asked, waving a newspaper.

"No, just the *Journal* this morning, and then I only glanced at it. Why?"

"Check this out. Recognize this guy? I know I've seen him before, maybe here at UNM." She pointed to a picture on the front page under a headline that announced PLANE CRASH PILOT IDENTIFIED. "You can have the paper. I gotta run. *Ciao!*" she said, scooting down the corridor.

Nena sat down and spread the paper out on her desk to get a better look at the photograph. She gasped aloud, as if someone had whacked the wind out of her. The pilot was identified as Charles LaCour, 27, an Albuquerque resident. She tried to swallow and found she couldn't. Her throat was dry, her breathing raspy and shallow as she stared at the gray, grainy image of Carlos, the smiling former student she had seen at the airport barely twenty-four hours ago. She put the newspaper down. Charles—Carlos—Chuck—LaCour—dead. Cheerful and handsome, and still so young. Now a lifeless corpse soon to be consigned to the earth. In the photo, he was standing under an apple tree. It didn't look like a professional shot. No doubt somebody who cared about him took it. A sister, a girlfriend, his father, a pal from the circle of his family and friends who were now grieving for him. Wondering why his plane had crashed. Wanting answers.

She picked up the newspaper and slowly read the story. A line at the beginning caught her attention. "Family members said LaCour was on his way to El Paso, where he was to be married this Saturday."

Tears welled in Nena's eyes. She remembered him telling her about getting married, explaining in fumbled Spanish *"Voy a casar mi amor."* He was so happy, so excited. What a tragedy, dying just days before his wedding. Surely his fiancée was deep in shock and grief. Maybe she took the photograph. Maybe she lived in El Paso, where the wedding would have taken place.

El Paso.

Strains of the conversation she overheard at customs the day before began to drift through her head. Hadn't those DEA guys mentioned something about El Paso?

". . . celebrate . . ."

". . . El Paso . . ."

"Chuckie's last drop . . ."

Charles LaCour . . . Chuck . . . Chuckie? It had to be a coincidence. She tried to clear her mind. No, there couldn't possibly be a connection.

6

Driving north toward Corrales and home, Nena put Linda Ronstadt's *Canciones de Mi Padre* into her truck's tape deck and cranked up the volume, hoping that the music, with its bouncy rhythms and soulful high held notes, would lift her spirits. But like a stuck record, her mind ceaselessly dwelled on LaCour's tragic death.

A half-hour later, Nena neared her house. Bouncing down Casey Boulevard, her truck's squeaky shocks protested the rough ride over the dirt road's gouges and gullies. She passed the trio of hulking old cottonwoods at the crossing of a lateral ditch and turned into the driveway of the adobe farmhouse her grandfather Casey left her. As usual, her barn cat Flaco waited for her by the back door, perched like an oversize furry orange gumdrop on the doormat that said GO AWAY.

As soon as she parked, the cat trotted over to the truck and meowed loudly, switching his tail back and forth.

"*¡Ay, gato!*" she groaned, tumbling out of the truck with an armload of books, papers, and her two-ton messenger bag. "I'll get you your dinner as soon as I can. You don't have to nag me!"

She unlocked the back door, stepped into her utility room, and dumped her things on top of the washing machine. Flaco brushed past her, heading for his food bowl. Suddenly he froze and let out a hiss so loud it made her jump, knocking her books to the floor. "*Jesús,* Flaco, you're going to give me a heart attack!" she cried as she picked them up.

The cat stood facing the kitchen with his back arched, his teeth bared, and his fur standing on end. A throaty, angry grrrrr boiled up from deep inside him. Nena stopped. Still growling, the cat whirled around, sped toward the open back door, and streaked away from the house in a blur of orange.

She carefully set the books down on the dryer and reached inside her bag for her pepper spray. A prickly sensation spread over her back and neck and down her arms. Gripping the spray dispenser, her finger trembling above the release button, she slowly walked into her kitchen. She looked into each corner, her heart throbbing in her throat. Nothing. She moved stealthily into the living room. The bank of house plants catching the last of the afternoon sun in the south-facing window, the red and black afghan heaped in her reading chair in front of the kiva fireplace—a quick glance said things appeared normal. Even if nothing felt normal.

She walked cautiously through the hallway, past the front door she never used and down the hall that led to the bedrooms, carefully examining each room, even peering under the beds. In the guest room, she slowly opened the folding door to the closet and found her summer wardrobe lying in a heap on the floor. In the bathroom, she swept the shower curtain aside and then checked the linen closet. She noticed the toilet seat was up. No one was hiding in the house, but somebody had definitely been there since she left home that morning. A male somebody. Nena felt her face and neck burn with outrage. She slammed down the toilet seat and washed her hands.

Taking several deep breaths, she returned to the utility room and put the pepper spray back in her purse. Slowly she went through the house again, reviewing everything. On this second, more thorough pass, she noticed things were ever so slightly out of place. The canned goods in the kitchen cupboard normally lined up at the front of the shelf were jumbled, some pushed forward, some back, some tipped over. In the living room, the neat piles of books and magazines on the huge old Pueblo drum that served as an end table by the sofa were a paper avalanche on the floor. A basket of smudge sticks had been dumped out onto the flat-topped leather trunk she used as a coffee table. Shreds of sage and cedar littered the surface. The folded sheets on her dresser and the books by her bedside were out of line. Whoever invaded her home had gone through everything in the house hastily, clumsily, looking for something.

Back in the living room, she saw that her Laura Gilpin photograph of La Bajada Hill was askew. An old friend of Laura's had traded it to Nena for an Ecuadorean necklace, and it was Nena's most prized possession. The brown paper backing on the photograph was slashed. The paper on all her other framed paintings, prints, photographs, and posters was also sliced open.

She re-hung the last picture in its place, stomped over to the telephone in the kitchen, and dialed her brother Luis. Before she called the police or did anything else, she had to talk to him. He and his wife Rose and their three children lived a short block down Casey Boulevard in the family homestead, a large, rambling adobe they had recently remodeled. After she punched in their number, Nena realized he wouldn't be home from work at his construction company yet. It was barely four.

7

"You sound kind of funny, Nena." Rose said when she answered. "Is everything okay?"

"Oh, I'm alright. Thanks. It was a long day at UNM. Listen, I'm sorry to bother you but would you ask Luis to come over as soon as he has a chance? I need him to, uh, check out my water heater. It's leaking again."

"Are you having phone problems?"

"No. Why?"

"Well, I saw a U.S. West truck parked by your back door this morning, not long after you left for class. I was just wondering."

Nena suddenly felt very cold. Could someone have tapped her phone? No, that was a stretch, she told herself. Why would anyone want to listen to her calls? "Uh, it seems all right," she said.

She poured herself a glass of wine. Her hand was shaking so badly that the bottle rattled against the rim of her glass, splattering red drops on the kitchen counter. She carried the glass carefully into the living room. To keep busy, she made a fire in the fireplace, hoping its warmth would ward off the chill that had invaded her bones. She settled into an armchair in front of the hearth to wait for Luis. Flaco scratched at the back door. She got up and let him in. The cat pranced over to his food bowl as if nothing had happened, and when he finished his dinner, he found her in front of the fire trying unsuccessfully to read a book. With a meow, he leaped up into her lap and made himself comfortable.

She put her book down and tried to warm herself at the fire as she absently stroked his fur. "So Flaco, who was in here? And why? What was he after?"

The cat responded with a low purr.

A knock at the back door made her jump.

"Hey, it's me, Coyota," Luis announced.

She ran to let him in and gave him a tight hug.

"What's this about your water heater? Didn't I fix the damn thing for good last weekend?"

"You did, 'mano. It's something else."

"Eee, let me guess. Your washing machine. Your dryer. The fuel pump on your *troca*. Your septic tank. Oh, no, it better not be your septic tank. I don't do windows, floors, or septic tanks!"

"No, everything's fine. I just didn't feel like talking to Rosita about this. No point in both of us being terrified. It's really weird, Luis."

"It's that *gavacho* you've been seeing. Oh, boy. This calls for a beer. Do you have any real beer? Or just that yuppie stuff? I poured two yards of concrete today and I'd even drink a Fat Tire if I had to."

"All I have is Noche Buena. Sorry it's not that pisswater Bud you swill. Since it's almost Christmas, maybe you'll stoop to drinking the western hemisphere's best beer."

Luis accepted a Noche Buena, and Nena refilled her wineglass. They sat in front of the fire and she told him about the break-in, about the slashed pictures, and the dropped clothes in her closet. Luis was shocked. "I've never heard of a burglary around here. Did you call the cops?"

"No. I wanted to talk to you first. Besides, you know who they'll send—Cousin Johnny. I don't want that cretin coming over here, crawling through my stuff, asking me dumb questions. Even his own father says he's a few beers short of a six-pack. Since nothing's been taken, maybe the Corrales police wouldn't even bother to send him."

"Nothing's missing? Huh. That's strange. In that case, I guess you're right about not calling the cops. Why bother? They might conclude you're a few short of a six-pack yourself." He laughed.

"The ickiest thing is that the guy left the toilet seat up."

"Oh, boy, now you're talking a major felony!"

Nena grimaced. "This isn't funny! It's very, very creepy!"

Luis nodded. "I know, I know. I'm only trying to cheer you up."

She told him about the U.S. West truck Rose had seen earlier.

"That's strange. Then again those guys are always hanging around, futzing with this or that." He picked up the telephone and listened for a few seconds. "There's a strong hum on it, but we get that at home, too."

"There's something else," Nena said. She took a deep breath and told him about the plane crash. About the pilot who'd been her student. "I was one of the last people to see Carlos alive. Maybe I'm a raving lunatic, but I think I heard things I wasn't meant to hear, a couple of DEA guys talking in the customs office while I was sitting outside the door sewing labels in a shipment of sweaters. It was shortly before the plane crash. I'm not sure what they were saying . . . "

Luis sipped his beer pensively and grew solemn. "Tell me exactly what you think you heard. Think hard. Concentrate."

With her eyes closed, Nena mentally put herself back in the old airport building, on the other side of the frosted glass door from the two DEA agents. Slowly and methodically, she repeated as many of the sentence fragments as she could recall.

When she spoke the rhyming phrases ". . . inhaled his last rail . . . kicked his last bale . . . told his last tale . . ." Luis groaned. "Ay, Coyota!"

"What does that mean?" Nena said. "I don't get it."

"I didn't know you were such an *inocente*. They were talking drugs."

"Drugs?"

"'Rail' meaning a line of cocaine, and 'bale' as in 'a bale of marijuana.' Drug runners used to "kick bales" of smuggled dope out of small planes over the Corrales Valley in the good ol' days of the Free New Mexican Air Force. A ground crew would pick them up, break them down, and bag 'em into small, saleable amounts. Not that I ever had anything to do with that."

"Oh, my God! Is that what Carlos was transporting—dope, not electronics parts?"

Luis shrugged. "Maybe."

"Shit! Shit! Shit!" Nena cried. "I'm positive one of the men in the customs office said 'we fix his tanks.' I'm almost certain of it! *¡Ay Dios santo!* Do you think they killed him?"

"Eee, Nena. Chill. Don't rush to conclusions." Luis rubbed his jaw, took a long draft of his beer, and stoked up the fire. "Feds. Oh, man. You haven't talked to anybody else about what you heard, have you?"

"No. You're the first."

"Okay, let's think this thing through. For now, let's keep it between you and me. You don't know for sure that LaCour was a drug runner. And you don't know if the conversation and the plane crash have anything to do with each another. You can't just run out and make accusations, especially about *federales*."

"Luis, sweetie, I'm not that dumb."

"I know, I know. It would be a very serious allegation, and

there could be heavy-duty repercussions for you. If you want to keep your import business going, those DEA guys and their customs pals are the last people you want to piss off. They could come down on you like a rain of sledgehammers and ruin your business in a heartbeat. We need to consider this all very carefully before we make any moves. Meanwhile, to be on the safe side, I'd be cautious about what I said over the phone. There's probably a good reason why the U.S. West truck was here this morning."

"What do you mean? Isn't it illegal to wiretap law abiding people?"

"You never know with feds. Maybe I can think of a buddy who could check your line out for you."

Nena shuddered. "Jesus! I'm really upset, Luis. I'm totally wigged out. I feel like centipedes are crawling all over me!"

"Come spend the night with us. You'll feel safer."

"No, but thank you." Nena said.

"I've got an extra gun if you want it."

"I do not want a gun. You know I hate guns. Thanks anyway."

"How about a dog? I've got an extra dog. Great watchdog."

"El Dompe? You've been trying to get rid of that worthless fleabag ever since Tony brought him home from the dump two years ago."

"Speaking of Tony—how about a kid? He'd love to live here with you."

"Thanks, but no thanks. I'm not in the market for a used teenager. Luis, why would anybody break into my house? What were they looking for? Everything's still here—even my Indian jewelry. That's usually the first thing they take."

"It's not like you own a lot of pawnables, except for the jewelry. Nobody would bother to swipe your ten-year-old TV, or your Radio Shack computer, or your toaster oven, or any of your bizarro books. They don't seem to have been after money, or they would have taken your coin jar. You probably don't have any drugs . . ."

Nena cleared her throat. "Well . . . uh. You know how Mom's arthritis has been bothering her?"

"Uh huh. Although I think she uses it for sympathy. Like when she thinks we aren't paying enough attention to her."

"There's this old New Mexican remedio Grandmother Libertad used to give to people with arthritis. I don't know if the person who went through the house found it or not."

Luis rolled his eyes. "What's this remedio, Nena—*cocaína?*"

"No—marijuana. You mix it with alcohol and rub it on the affected joints."

"So to speak . . ."

"Smartass! It's really supposed to help, by numbing the pain, I guess. I wonder if they found it. It was in the medicine cabinet over the sink in the bathroom. I'll go see if it's still there." Nena disappeared and came out with a small baggie. "I guess they didn't find it," she said, opening the bag under her brother's nose. "I had it in a Band-Aid tin."

Luis sniffed the marijuana. "Ah, the sweet scent of my debauched youth along the Corrales clear ditch—what I remember of it, anyway. My baby sister, a pothead! Who would have guessed? Where'd you get the dope, Coyota?"

"There's a grad student in the art department who's a small time dealer. It's not for me, Luis, honest. It's for Mom. I was going to mix it with alcohol and put it in a pretty bottle and give it to her for Christmas. I probably shouldn't have it in the house, though. Maybe I should hide it on the ditchbank."

"I'll take care of it for you. I built a couple of first-class hidey-holes into our house, including one Rosita doesn't know about. If she finds it, though, you'll have to help me convince her it's yours, not mine or Tony's, agreed?"

Nena nodded.

Luis pocketed the baggie. "You know who could help you with all this? Call Ruben."

She sighed. "That's long over, Luis. You know that."

"I hear he's a detective now, and he's on a federal task force. A rising star in the Albuquerque Police Department."

She stared at the floor. "Isn't he getting married?"

"Nope. The way I heard, that got called off. I'm not sure by who. Hey—I'm not saying you have to get back together with him. Just go talk to him, Nena. He's *gente,* one of us. He knows you, and you can trust him completely. I know you didn't dream up what you heard, or this house break-in thing either. And so will he. And more important, he knows how the feds work." Luis stood up and set down his empty beer bottle on the fireplace. "Think about it."

Nena got out of her chair, put her arms around him, and rested her head on his shoulder.

"You're sure you're going to be okay alone tonight?" he asked.

"I'm fine. Thanks." She stood on tiptoes, kissed his cheek, and let him out into the dark night, locking the door carefully behind him.

8

As she listened to the crunch of Luis's departing footfalls, Nena leaned against the kitchen counter and considered his advice. Her brother meant well, but there was no way she was going to talk to Ruben Abeyta about what she heard at the customs office—or about anything else.

Ruben and Nena had been friends since they were undergraduates at UNM. After nine years together they even talked about getting married. The main obstacle was Ruben's widowed mother, who seemed to do everything possible to keep Nena and her son apart. She was a raging hypochondriac who ate antibiotics like candy, and demanded painkillers and tranquilizers from a squadron of obliging physicians. Over the years, her health obsessions intensified. Ruben, her only child, spent a lot of his free time ferrying her from one doctor's appointment to another, yet there rarely was anything wrong with her. Perhaps fearing she was losing him to Nena, she announced that she was dying of an unspecified illness, and demanded that Ruben move back home to care for her. He gave up his apartment and obeyed.

Nena understood his loyalty, yet she also noticed that whenever she and Ruben made plans to be together for awhile—to leave town for a weekend, to work on her house—his mother's condition worsened and he had to cancel their plans. Hurt and mystified by the hold Mrs. Abeyta had on her son, Nena grew resentful.

On her thirtieth birthday, as she and Ruben were sitting down to a special dinner he had cooked for her, his mother called. The old woman was deaf and spoke loudly. Nena could hear the conversation from the other side of the room.

"*¡Hijito!* You must come home now and take me to the hospital. It's my heart. It feels like knives in my chest!"

"Mom, are you sure it isn't indigestion like the last time?"

"No, *hijo,* it's a heart attack! Come now! Imagine how you'll feel if you come home and find me lying dead on the kitchen floor!"

As Ruben tried to reason with his mother, Nena sat glumly clutching her napkin and watching the food grow cold. Tears came to her eyes. He hung up the phone, came around her chair from behind, put his hands on her shoulders, and buried his face in her hair. "You don't have to explain," she said. "Go."

Ruben returned several hours later, to find Nena already in bed. He approached her bedside. "*¿Amorcito?*" he called out softly.

She pretended to be asleep, afraid of what she might say to him in anger or hurt. He left the bedroom. She listened as he put away the uneaten food in the kitchen. He walked out the door, closing it gently behind him. She heard his police sedan rumbling slowly down the road.

The following weekend, he took her out to dinner at Seasons Grill in Old Town for a belated birthday celebration and presented her with a beautiful pair of antique turquoise earrings she knew had cost him a fortune. Later at her house, they were happily making slow, luxurious love for the first time in weeks when the phone began to ring. It was well past midnight.

"Let it ring," Ruben mumbled.

"No, I can't," Nena said. "Nobody ever calls me this late. It has to be important." She picked up the receiver. It was Ruben's mother. Wordlessly, Nena handed him the phone.

"Hijito, I have to go to the emergency room!" his mother yelled. "I think it's appendicitis!"

"Mom, you had your appendix out before you married Pops."

"Then it's another thing! Maybe a tumor! I'm scared, *m'hijo*. My side—it hurts like it's on fire! If you're too busy to come, I can call the ambulance and go to the hospital alone."

"No, Mom, I'll be right there."

✳   ✳   ✳   ✳   ✳

The next day, Nena asked Ruben to meet her after his shift ended at three. He drove up to her house and found her standing in the driveway, waiting for him. "I've had it!" she cried as he got out of his car. "You need to either tell your mother to see a psychiatrist, or get a new girlfriend! I'm not a yo-yo! I love you, but how can I compete with a crazy old lady? Shit, I don't want to compete with her. I simply want to have a peaceful, private relationship with the man I love."

Ruben sighed. "She's lonely, Nena. I'm all she's got."

"I know that. We've been over this a million times. She knows exactly how and when to push my buttons—and yours. I'm sorry. I can't go on like this!"

"Nena, don't ask me to choose between you and Mom."

"I wouldn't dream of it. I'll make the decision for you. Good bye! And I mean it! Go home to your mother." Hiding her tears, she fled into her house.

✳   ✳   ✳   ✳   ✳

A few days after she broke up with Ruben, his mother did have a heart attack. She had a triple bypass, and was hospitalized for weeks. Nena felt terrible when Luis told her. "Why didn't he call me? Pride? Machismo? Anger?" she ranted to her brother. "Was our relationship so shallow he couldn't tell me his mother truly was ill?"

"So call him, Nena," Luis said.

"I will not," she said. "I'm not going back to playing second fiddle to her!"

"It's a damn good thing you're not stubborn," Luis said, shaking his head.

"I'd almost swear she had that heart attack on purpose," she said.

9

Nena stood in her living room and surveyed the improvements she and Ruben had made to her house together—the oiled *vigas,* the re-plastered walls, the brick floors repaired and leveled. A house she thought they would share some day. A house that had now been violated by unknown intruders. She shivered. Her home was cold and alien to her. Nena had never felt so alone.

"Oh, Grandmother Libertad, I wish you were here!" she said plaintively in a child's tiny voice, calling on her *abuelita,* who died when Nena was ten.

Nena spent her early years traipsing after her paternal grandmother, a wizened slip of a woman, silent as a summer wind. She lived behind the Casey house in a one-room adobe, her only companions a black cat that sunned itself on the windowsill and her doting granddaughter. Together, Nena and Libertad wandered the sandhills and the bosque along the river in search of herbs and roots the old woman used for curing the pains and ills of the many people who came to her for help. They were inseparable.

After Nena found her granny dead in her rocking chair in front of the window, no one in the Casey family grieved more than she did.

She never told anyone, but sometimes Libertad still visited her—not as a human figure, per se, rather as a sudden breeze that slipped over Nena like silk, a whiff of wild herbs and wet earth, the creaking of Libertad's rocking chair in her bedroom.

Nena knew exactly what her abuela would have her do to

recover her home's peace. She picked up one of the smudge sticks from the coffee table, a tubular bundle of cedar and sage sprigs wrapped with red string, a smudge stick she made as Libertad had taught her. She closed her eyes and held it tightly in her fist. She breathed deeply for several minutes to calm herself, then opened her eyes. She fetched matches from the fireplace, and walking into the farthest corner of her bedroom, she lit the tip of the bundle of herbs. As smoke curled upward, she drew it toward herself with a cupped hand, spreading it over her body, and breathing it deep into her lungs. She passed the bundle through the air in the corners and recesses of each room, letting the fragrant smoke cleanse the dwelling and get rid of the evil that had invaded it.

Her ritual completed, a peace settled over Nena. Her house, redolent of the clean-edged scent of sage and cedar, felt like home again, her refuge, her safe place. She sat back down in front of the hearth, gathered Flaco into her arms, and held him close. For hours, she stared into the fire, her mind a blank slate.

Eventually, she drifted back to the present. As tiny flames stroked the undersides of the last logs, Nena reflected on how Cal might react to her doing her "Indian" thing with the smudge stick, and she smiled. They probably didn't do things like that back in Rhode Island, and not just because they didn't have sagebrush handy. Cal would think it was ridiculous and superstitious, but she didn't care. It worked for her.

10

Although she went to bed feeling relaxed and comforted, Nena's dreams were convoluted and violent. She was running through a cactus-studded desert in the dark, approaching a narrow bridge. Unknown evil people were after her, intent on harming her, and she had to run as fast as she could to evade them. In the morning, she could only recall vague outlines of the nightmare. Dawn was breaking. The sun, a plump yellow egg yolk, rose from behind the dark, opaque Sandías. She rolled out of bed and hunted up her cold-weather running gear.

The mid-December day was bright and unseasonably mild over the Valley. Inca doves cooed from their perches on telephone wires, and flickers called out to each other as they swooped between cottonwood branches and fence posts. Pairs of Mexican mallards whirred through a sky that was stretched like turquoise taffeta behind wispy sweeps of white clouds.

At the end of the driveway, Nena stooped to tighten the laces of her running shoes as a V of Canadian geese approached from the south, heading toward the river, flying so low over the Russian olive trees along Casey Boulevard that she could almost feel the fanning of their wings through the still air. She straightened up and watched them drop from sight beyond the treetops of the bosque. The clear, fresh morning air was quickly dissolving the lingering miasma of her nightmares.

As she trotted down the ditchbank, she wanted the day to be

like any other—normal, new, open-ended, safe. Since LaCour's death, the world Nena thought she knew made far less sense than before. Feeling adrift and unsure of where she fit into this new reality, she decided to anchor herself to those aspects of her life over which she had a measure of control. Her daily jog was a good place to begin. As she had every morning for years, she padded methodically along the ditch, focusing on the path ahead, placing one foot firmly in front of the other, a routine that could serve as a metaphor for how she would deal with the future—one step at a time.

When she reached the farthest point of her usual route, she saw a man sitting in a white Ford Taurus parked a half-block down the street. She remembered the car crossing the acequia earlier. Although he was too far away for her to see his features clearly, his pale face was trained on her. Nena glared at him. He started his engine and drove off. "Hmmmm," she thought. "Lost? Another real estate speculator checking out the neighborhood? A pervert?"

Several blocks later, where another dirt road traversed the ditch, the Taurus reappeared on the opposite bank. She caught a fleeting glimpse of the man behind the wheel. He was black-haired, middle-aged, bearded, wearing a dark colored jacket and sunglasses. He grinned at her menacingly, and driving slowly, he began to pace her. Her heart beat faster. With determination she sped up, her teeth clenched, her eyes drilled into the far-off western horizon, her hands balled up into fists. No more than forty feet from her, the Taurus deliberately matched her pace, the driver flicking his attention between the road ahead and Nena, his smile malevolent and threatening. Whatever his game was, she wanted no part of it.

Rounding a curve, she quickly slipped behind a stand of

huge cottonwoods and ran as fast as she could down a narrow trail through the sagebrush that led to the old cemetery. Behind her, she heard the car accelerate. He was probably heading for the nearest intersection two blocks away. She smiled to herself. "He'll never be able to follow me now." She vaulted the low rock wall, ran past graves new and old decorated with fading plastic flowers, ducked behind the old church, and made her way home via a labyrinth of hidden lateral ditches and dirt paths she knew like the palm of her hand.

She reached her driveway, picked up the newspaper, and continued into the house. Doing her best to forget about the man who followed her, she went deliberately through her morning routine, setting out food for Flaco, and putting oatmeal to cook slowly while she showered and dressed. She sat down to a leisurely, normal breakfast. When she picked up the *Journal,* though, she found herself searching for a follow-up story about the plane crash. At the bottom of the second page of the B section, a headline mentioned the accident: PLANE CRASH MAY HAVE BEEN SUICIDE. Nena nearly fainted. In horrified disbelief, she read on.

> Authorities at Albuquerque International Airport suspect that Charles LaCour, the pilot of a single-engine Cessna that crashed south of the airport on Wednesday, may have intentionally killed himself. LaCour's parents, Evelyn and Roger LaCour of Albuquerque, and the pilot's fiancée, Justine Fischer of El Paso, adamantly dispute the suicide contention. "We demand a full investigation of the crash," said Roger LaCour. "My son was not suicidal. He was about to marry a young woman he loved."

Tears ran down Nena's cheeks as she slowly folded the newspaper. She vehemently hoped LaCour's family would succeed in finding out why their son died. Couldn't she find a way to help them without putting herself at risk?

She glanced at the kitchen clock. She had to leave for town to keep her appointment with La Ñapa, even if she wasn't in the mood for selling things. Need beckoned.

11

Nena parked in front of La Ñapa's pitched-roof Victorian adobe. Her friend Pancha Archibeque managed the Latin American imports store and often bought stock from her. When Pancha saw Nena struggling with the awkward carton of sweaters and Christmas ornaments she came out to help her carry it inside.

"It's at times like these that I envy diamond merchants." Nena said as they set the heavy box down in the office at the rear of the building. "All your inventory could fit into a matchbox."

"Yeah?" Pancha laughed. "What if you dropped the matchbox down a sewer grate?"

"At least you wouldn't have to take inventory at the end of the year, would you?"

As Pancha picked through the sweaters for a variety of sizes and styles, Nena explained the terms she could offer La Ñapa. "I know it's awfully late in the season, so I'm happy to give the sweaters to you on consignment. Fifty-fifty, rather than the usual sixty-forty. Same with the Christmas ornaments. Sell what you can, and I'll come get the rest after the holidays. The damn shipment didn't arrive until Wednesday, and I had to sit there and sew labels in all forty chompas before customs would let me have them."

"You're lucky they let you do that," Pancha said, pulling a sweater over her head and fumbling for the sleeves to check the fit. "They confiscated part of a small shipment of ours from Guatemala a few weeks ago."

"Why? What was in it?"

"Two dozen of those little embroidered velvet drawstring bags. They said they needed to determine the fiber content. Fat lot of good those bags'll do us next July when their textile expert in El Paso gets through inspecting them. We could have sold them all by now. They're perfect evening purses for the holidays."

"What's customs' problem? The velvet is a synthetic. Probably acetate. Who cares? All the synthetics pay the same duty, I think. And besides, they're handmade. Cottage industry, not industrial goods. They shouldn't be affected by the textile quotas."

"Believe me, I tried all the arguments, and it did no good. I think they're just out to hassle my boss again."

Nena frowned. "They're still bothering Beverly? Haven't they given it up by now?"

"Nope. It's been almost ten years since she blew that customs agent out of the water for being in cahoots with drug lords, and his colleagues are on her case to this day. Even though nobody liked him and he was convicted on corruption charges. She's so pissed off she's writing a book about it. In fact, she's off in Mexico for a month, working on it."

"Good for her. What a *güevonada!* She sure has brass balls. I hope she really socks it to them, the *pinche cabrones!* I mean, not all those people are bozos. I get along well enough with Bisbee . . ."

"He's the one who confiscated the embroidered bags."

"Really? I considered him a regular guy."

"As far as I can tell, none of 'em are okay if they think their imperial institution is threatened. And I guess there's no bigger threat to those macho assholes than successful, uppity women like Beverly. She's got their number and she's willing to stand up to them."

Nena was silent. On her way into town she considered the idea of going to Clark Bisbee about the DEA guys' conversation. He was the customs officer she most trusted. The two other inspectors were morons. But she knew Pancha was right. And Luis, too. She would be a fool to go to anybody in customs. Federales all covered each other's asses. The next thing she knew, they'd harass her big-time like they did Beverly Parmentier, a decent, on-the-level businesswoman respected by everybody in the trade.

Well, there were still other agencies she might talk to. According to the paper, the National Transportation Safety Board was investigating the crash. There were also the FBI and the Albuquerque police. But how could she be sure they wouldn't go right back to the DEA with what she told them?

Pancha and Nena settled on the inventory list as two bland, crew-cut young men in leather jackets with military insignia sauntered through the front door. Pancha went to greet them.

One walked back to the office, leaned against the doorframe, and watched Nena pack the reject sweaters back into the box. His companion was keeping Pancha busy up front with questions about La Ñapa's sources for vintage pottery. "Whatcha got there?" he asked, cracking his gum, his hands shoved into the front pockets of his tight jeans.

"A box of Cruise missiles," Nena said.

"Heh, heh. No, really."

"Cachibachis," she replied, using the term for "whatevers."

"Looks like sweaters to me. Where're they from?"

"Upper Volta," Nena said, scooping up the box and sweeping

past him. At the front of the store, she leaned the carton against the counter and murmured to Pancha, *"¿Está bién si te dejo con estos pendejos?* Will you be alright alone with these jerks? I have to get to class."

Pancha smiled. *"No te preocupes. Ya estoy acostumbrada, carnala. Gracias.* I'll be fine, I'm used to them."

"Yeah," Nena thought as she trundled the box toward her truck, "Pancha's probably an expert at handling those government creeps by now. How those idiots ever thought anyone would believe they were real customers is beyond comprehension. Or maybe they don't care. Maybe they even want to be obvious. It's hard to second guess swine."

12

That afternoon, Nena was collecting exam papers from the last few students when Cal stopped by her classroom.

"Free for a cuppa java?" he asked.

She smiled. "Sure. Let me dump these in my office first. I'll see you at Café Olé."

A quarter-hour later, she found Cal at their usual table in the corner. She set her coffee cup down, dropped her bag into a vacant chair, and sat down next to him.

He leaned over and kissed her. "So where in Mexico are we going?" he asked, wrapping his long tapered fingers around a glass of steamy latte.

"You're serious about going to Mexico?"

"Of course! If you're really willing to be my tour guide and translator?"

"*Claro.*"

"I assume that's an affirmative."

She nodded yes and smiled. "Your Spanish lessons are about to begin."

Cal groaned. "I have to admit I'm not very good at foreign languages. Let's get together over the weekend for a planning session—in English, of course. Dinner at my place tomorrow night?"

"Great. I'll bring a salad, if you'd like. I'm doing the flea market tomorrow, so between that and correcting finals, I won't be able to actually cook anything."

"A salad would be excellent. For a main course, I might whip up a batch of *petits oiseaux sans têtes* for us. How does that sound?"

"Small headless birds?" Nena was skeptical. "You know, I could pick us up a couple of orders of *carne adovada* at the Sanitary Tortilla Factory, Cal. It wouldn't be a problem."

He gasped. Cal hated "spicy" food. He reached across the table to pat her hand. "Veal *paupiettes*, Nena. No actual ornithology involved."

She smiled. She wasn't sure what paupiettes were, but she knew what veal was. Whenever she saw it listed on a menu, she automatically envisioned the pitiable sight of little motherless Holsteins cooped up in plastic doghouses awaiting their doom. Well, just this once she'd make an exception for Cal.

13

Saturday morning, Nena skipped her jog and left home early to be at the Albuquerque fairgrounds by seven, hoping to secure a prime spot for her flea market stall.

"Ms. Herrera-Casey, how are you this fine morning?" asked the gatekeeper, a retired Irish firefighter.

"Great, Seamus. And yourself?"

"Couldn't be better. Are you wanting your usual accommodations?"

"You bet! Row three, between the Padillas and Jake, if that space is still available."

"Indeed it is," he said. "That'll be seven dollars."

Nena drove through the gate and pulled her truck into her preferred slot.

"¡Buenos días!" José Padilla called out to her. He and his wife, Gertrudis, were an elderly couple from Los Lunas who sold honey, apples, cider, and Valencia County peanuts out of the back of their battered 1954 Apache pick-up. Jake, the grizzled, bowlegged cowboy to the other side of Nena's space, winked and wished her a good morning, too. His double-sized stand was piled higher than usual with heaps of used clothing, country and western tapes and CD's, tools, and cases of Indian jewelry.

Nena set up two collapsible banquet tables in an L-shape, and laid out neat piles of Ecuadorean sweaters, straw Christmas ornaments, weavings, baskets, twined bags, wooden masks, market toys, and the other Latin American merchandise that comprised her inventory.

The Albuquerque flea market was quintessential New Mexico. Many of the vendors were semi-permanent fixtures like Nena and her neighbors, who held regular jobs during the week, but appeared at "The Flea" every weekend to supplement their income. Others were closet-cleaners, homeowners spending a Saturday or Sunday selling off things they didn't need any more—baby gear, crockery, snow tires, yard tools, broken radios, and other cast-offs. They spread their offerings on an old blanket on the ground or sold out of the open trunk of a sedan.

As the sun crept above the dark elephant gray hump of the Sandías, brightening the December morning and warming the air, customers began to dawdle over Nena's goods. Like the sellers, the buyers were a mix, from the pony-tailed Santa Fe set in their Beacon blanket coats to the hatless and gloveless poor in threadbare army surplus jackets. Early bird, eagle-eyed professional pickers scoured amateurs' card tables and blankets for the valuable old Indian pots, Taxco silver, war souvenirs, and genuine antiques that showed up now and then. Pueblo Indians offered to trade strands of turquoise or melon-shell beads for household goods. Giggling young couples wandered around on informal dates. Navajo cowboys came in from the reservation for a weekend on the town. Immigrants strolled through a lively, colorful open-air market that perhaps reminded them of markets at home in Africa, Asia, or Latin America.

Sipping coffee from her thermos and prancing in place on the toes of her lined boots to keep warm, Nena greeted potential customers and talked up her wares. "Good morning! How about a beautiful, hand-knit sweater? For cheap! Warm, water-resistant, natural handspun wool. No dyes. A great Christmas present! Could I interest you in these antique Andean weavings?"

A potential buyer began to sort through the brightly striped jute bags. "These are *shigras*," Nena said. "Indians in the Ecuador highlands use them to carry produce. They make wonderful, sturdy handbags. Jute fiber."

"I know," the woman said. "I bought one myself in Ecuador. Your prices are very fair, nearly what I paid in Quito."

"Thank you," Nena said. "I do my best to offer my things for as little as possible."

The woman picked out two shigras. "These are for my daughters' Christmas presents. They're always threatening to steal mine."

Nena wrote up the sale, took the woman's money, and handed her the bags. "Christmas ornaments, anyone?" she called out to passers-by. "Straw ones woven by the very same Indians in Ecuador who make the famous Panama hats. How about a Panama hat? Summer's just around the corner!"

Some people were interested. Others wanted to know the prices, even though all but the smallest items had price tags. A neatly-coiffed brunette in a full-length fox fur coat flipped the tag of an Ecuadorean sweater. "Ninety dollars for zis?" she scoffed in German-accented English. "You probably paid ten dollars for zat in Guatemala, taking advantage of zos poor Indians."

Nena gave the woman a phony smile. "The sweater's from Ecuador, and I paid the knitting cooperative members their asking price, as always. This is the same sweater that Ralph Lauren sells for four hundred dollars. Yours for less than a fourth of his price!"

The woman sniffed and meandered off.

"Rich bitch," Jake muttered under his breath. "Y'know, the more money they got, the more snot they got," he said.

"You sure have to have a thick skin to work this place," Mrs. Padilla said. "People like that lady are downright rude! I'm a knitter, and I can tell you there's more than fifty dollars worth of wool in that sweater. Handspun!"

"You sure can't let yourself be bothered by cheapskates, that's for sure," Mr. Padilla chimed in. "I've been in this business for an eternity, and I decided years ago there's a difference between poor people and cheap people. Poor people have dignity—or at least they don't call attention to their lack of money by complaining about prices. Cheap people are downright tight with the money they've got, and they often have plenty."

"Right you are," Jake said. "Now them rich people, what they want is to think they got the better of you in the deal, so they do their goldarndest to beat you down on prices. They may not even want what they're haggling over; they just want to win."

Nena and the Padillas agreed.

By eleven, she had sold dozens of Christmas ornaments and other small goods, plus a weaving, the two shigras, and six sweaters. The mid-December day was turquoise bright, with snow on the Sandías and enough of a chill to lend a festive air to the market's ambiance. Many vendors had decorated their stands with plastic evergreen branches or blinking Christmas lights, and from all corners of the market, holiday music blared from radios and boomboxes.

In the booth to Nena's right, Jake played Willie Nelson's *Pretty Paper* Christmas album. When the old cowboy wanted to fight off the cold or drum up business, he jangled a string of brass sleigh bells hanging from a corner of his truck and bounced up and down, piercing the air with exuberant ho! ho! ho!'s. Nena smiled to herself. She knew at least part of the vaquero's holiday cheer was being stoked by the bottle of Jack Daniels he kept handy under his jewelry table.

14

Down the aisle, unnoticed by Nena, a tall, wide-shouldered, brown-skinned man in a crimson and white UNM letter jacket stood by strands of bright red chile *ristras,* sorting through rusty gardening tools set out on a plank table. Next to him, the booth tender and a man holding an expensive-looking gold and gem bracelet in his fist conversed in low whispers. Feigning interest in the tools, the man in the letter jacket listened in on their conversation. That was his job. It was difficult to hear what they were saying above the flea market din and the holiday music blaring from competing speakers. As he tilted his head slightly and moved closer to the men in an effort to get a better look at the bracelet, he caught sight of a familiar, raven-haired woman leaning over her makeshift counter to give a sweater to a customer. He held his breath.

Things had been going fairly well for Ruben Abeyta. After ten years as a policeman, he was recently made a detective with the Albuquerque Police Department. He got a raise, he now had better hours, and both the quality of the people he worked with and his assignments had improved. Since his mother's death two years before, he busied himself remodeling the South Valley home where he spent his childhood. He put in skylights to lighten the dark interior and replaced her fussy, timeworn furniture with his own things.

Ruben missed his mother. She went steadily downhill after

bypass surgery. When she failed to wake up one morning, he was greatly relieved that her ordeal was over. But then he felt guilty that he was relieved.

Lifting weights, running, and playing softball helped him stay fit at two-twenty, good fighting weight for a tall, large-boned man. Yet there was something missing in Ruben's life, and her name was Nena Herrera-Casey. The woman he once hoped to marry. The woman he'd lost through his poor, neurotic, and lonely mother's jealousy, and his own mishandling of the situation.

Ruben shifted his weight from one foot to another and tried to concentrate on the conversation. The man holding the bracelet was a known thief with a thirty-year heroin habit, and the prospective buyer was a fence APD was trying to nail. In spite of this Ruben couldn't help glancing Nena's way now and then.

*   *   *   *   *

Nena was rummaging in the back of her truck for more sweaters when someone called out her name. Looking up, she saw a sallow man with long greasy hair dangling from under a knit watch cap. He was flipping through her neat piles of sweaters.

"Nice shit," he said sniffling. "Could I interest you in a trade?" He studied her with large, rheumy eyes. It was the grad student, Nena remembered. In the art department. The one who sold her the dope for her mother's remedio.

Out of the corner of her eye, she saw a man who was talking to the Padillas aim a camcorder at her and the art student and shoot a few seconds of film. Before she could protest, Jake yelled, "Hey!" and she saw a kid speed away from her booth past Jake's, tucking a couple of her Bolivian weavings into his jacket.

"Watch my stuff for me, will you?" she called out to the student and took off running after the thief. Jake was shouting down the lane for people to stop the kid, but he was fast and quickly blended into the thick crowd. Nena wove in and out of the clusters of shoppers, soon losing sight of the boy. At the end of the row she stopped, not knowing whether he had gone left or right. Now worried about the rest of her inventory, she jogged back to her space. "Dammit!" she said to no one in particular as she tried to figure out what was missing.

"What did he get?" Jake asked.

"I think only two weavings. Of course they were my most expensive ones. Really fine aguayos—a Bolivian Potolo-region weaving and a Cusco vegetal dye. *¡Carajo!* Well, I wish him luck trying to fence textiles for anything. Damn, damn, damn!"

The art student eyed her. "Uh, I know it's probably not a good time for you," he said sniffling. "But are you interested in a deal? I have some first-rate merchandise for the holidays."

"No, it's not a good time for me," Nena replied curtly. "Goddamn it! How about you go find that kid for me?" As soon as she asked the question, she could see he had no desire to help her, which annoyed her even more. "Forget it," she said. "And to answer your question, no, I'm not interested in any deals. Especially now. Sorry if I'm being rude. That was a huge loss."

She felt on the verge of tears. Of anger or sorrow—she wasn't sure which.

"Maybe it's not such a big loss after all," he said, nodding down the row of vendors, whose heads were turned toward a powerfully-built man in a red and white jacket striding purposefully toward Nena's booth, a huge hand clamped firmly on the arm of a squirming, scrawny kid. She recognized the big man and her heart felt like it had been dropped onto dry ice. His eyes met hers and a broad grin spread over his leathery face.

"Merry Christmas, María Azucena," Ruben said. He handed her the missing weavings. "Is this your thief?"

Nena managed a smile, but couldn't speak. She nodded.

"That's him! That's the little fucker!" Jake yelled. "I seen him take them weavings. Yessir, that's the little shit all right!"

"Do you want to press charges, Nena?"

"Yes, Ruben, I do. Those weavings are worth three hundred apiece. And all of us here are tired of getting ripped off. I think somebody's got these kids organized to steal from us. It's like *Oliver Twist* all over again."

Ruben nodded. "Yeah, that's what we think, too. We've been on the lookout for Fagan all year," he joked. "I'll call a patrol car."

The boy, who was about nine or ten, began to kick at Ruben's legs. "Ow, you're hurting my arm, man! Lemme go! I didn't steal nothing! Them weavings ain't worth no six hundred bucks. Fuck you, bitch!"

Ruben sighed heavily and tucked the kid tightly under his arm as if he were a football. "I'll be back in a bit. Don't go anywhere," he said.

Nena smiled. "I'll be right here."

Half an hour later, Ruben returned. "We'll have to keep the weavings for a while as evidence. Is that a problem?"

"No. As long as I get a receipt for them. They're hard to sell, and anyway, maybe I shouldn't have such valuable stuff out here. I guess I should feel sorry for that kid. He's probably had a rotten life, and it's not going to get any better for him in juvenile detention."

"Now and then, kids actually do get the help they need while they're in the j.d. home. You might be doing him a favor."

"I hope so." She gazed up at the detective. "You're looking good, Ruben. Younger, not older than the last time I saw you. I'd like to know your secret."

"I didn't feel too young chasing down that *chamaco,* I'll tell you. He was a fast little son of a gun."

"You saw him take the weavings?"

"I saw him running away from your booth carrying something so I took out after him."

Nena regarded the detective carefully. "Were you watching me, guy?"

He briefly turned aside to hide his smile. "Uh, no. Although I am sort of here on business. Which reminds me . . ."

He glanced around quickly to see if anyone was standing close by and stepped nearer to Nena before speaking softly. "I'd be careful about doing any business with that long-haired grease-ball who was checking out your sweaters when the kid made his grab. He's a sleazy, two-bit dope dealer. And a snitch."

Nena straightened up and stepped back. "I wasn't doing any business with him, Ruben, especially not any funny business, if that's what you're implying."

"I wasn't implying anything, Nena. Give me a break. I'm your friend."

"Uh huh," she said, folding her arms over her chest, glaring at him.

Ruben studied her carefully with his large brown eyes, then looked off into the distance. "I wish you'd talk to me," he said.

Nena's stomach tightened. "I never said I wouldn't talk to you. You just never asked. And . . . well, maybe it's too late now."

The instant she said it might be too late, she regretted it. Why was it too late?

Ruben nodded, his jaw set. "Yeah, maybe you're right. Well, see you around," he said abruptly.

Before she knew it, he'd dissolved into the throng and was gone.

*　　*　　*　　*　　*

When Ruben returned to the booth where he'd been ostensibly inspecting garden tools, the man with the bracelet had disappeared. There was no way of knowing whether or not a transaction had taken place, and Ruben hadn't really heard enough of the conversation to get a search warrant on the probable fence. He walked down the aisles dejectedly. Maybe another day.

His encounter with María Azucena didn't make him feel any better. She was lovelier than ever, and it ached to look at her. He was happy he was able to recover her weavings, but the effort didn't seem to have gotten him enough points so she would sit down and talk to him. The kind of heart to heart talk that was years overdue. Friday nights, when Ruben joined Nena's brother and the other guys to play poker, Luis kept counseling him to call her up or drop in on her at home.

"I wish you two would get back together again," he said more than once.

Ruben never got up the courage to contact her. He didn't think she would talk to him, and he also didn't think he could bear her rejection.

As he made his way through the flea market to the parking lot and his cruiser, Ruben remembered the scene where the kid snatched Nena's weavings. His detective's mind was nettled by the man filming Nena in her booth right before the boy took off running. Ruben was quite certain the man was in his handcuffing seminar last year at Kirtland Air Force Base. Why was he filming Nena? Maybe it was the art student he was interested in. The man was a known drug dealer. That made sense.

15

Although her heart was no longer into selling, Nena stayed at the fairgrounds for another couple of hours. People were in the mood for Christmas shopping, and her lack of enthusiasm wasn't enough to stop them from buying another half-dozen sweaters and more than a hundred dollars' worth of Christmas decorations. By the time she packed her wares into their boxes, folded the tables, and shoved everything back into the Toyota, she had sales of almost fifteen hundred dollars. The Ecuador shipment, including freight, landing costs, and duties, was now paid for. And she hadn't lost her weavings after all. It was one of her best flea market days ever.

Ordinarily, she would have been ecstatic, singing along with Linda Ronstadt on her way home. But as she drove toward Corrales, she found herself in tears. "Goddamn that Ruben!" She pounded the steering wheel, anger swirling through her brain like a dust devil. "The minute I think I'm finally over him and he's gone from my life forever, he pops up again like a jack-in-the-box! I will never, ever let him hurt me again."

Once she was home, she made herself a cup of tea and curled up in her overstuffed armchair in front of the fireplace. Flaco warmed her lap.

For a long while, she regarded the cold ashes of the previous fire through a wash of tears. Thinking about Ruben brought back all the anger and sorrow of the innumerable times he'd let her down. Was the Ruben who saved her weavings at the flea market the same man who promised her again and again that he would talk his mother into seeing a counselor about her health obsessions? The man who left her sitting alone on countless occasions because his mother demanded he come home and take care of her?

Then she remembered the good times and why she fell in love with him in the first place. His goodness. His laconic sense of humor. His warmth and his strength. The beautiful way he made love to her. Ruben was the man she once wanted to be her life partner and the father of her children.

As soon as she learned about his mother's death, Nena sent him flowers and a heartfelt note, expecting to hear from him eventually. He never called. A year after they broke up, Luis told her Ruben was seeing a woman he dated in high school and hinted that they seemed serious.

"Luis, I don't want to hear about Ruben. It's over! He made his choice, and I made mine."

But the news stung. Maybe it was a final nail in the coffin in which she had buried all her hopes for reconciliation. She refused to let herself think about him. It all hurt too much. Maybe seeing Cal was a start in the right direction.

Cal! Nena leaped to her feet, sending Flaco into a surprised tumble. She ran into the kitchen to check the clock. She had barely enough time to throw together a salad and change clothes before heading for his house. Although now she would rather spend the evening at home with her cat and a novel, it was too late to call him with an excuse.

16

"Sorry I'm late," Nena said when Cal opened the door of his Mission-style bungalow near the university.

"Au contraire. Your timing is excellent, my dear," he replied, giving her a pouty kiss. He took the salad bowl from her arms and helped her out of her coat sweater. "The paupiettes are almost done, and so is the wild rice pilaf."

As Cal skillfully finished the dinner preparations, Nena recounted her day at the flea market. He opened a bottle of Nouveau Beaujolais and poured it into glasses. "It seems you're in a risky business, dear. What a stroke of fortune for your policeman friend to appear on the scene."

Nena was glad Cal had his back to her. She took a deep breath and let it out slowly as she watched him artfully arrange the steaming food on the plates.

"He's not really a friend—he's a guy I went to college with," she said, tucking a stray strand of hair behind her ear. "He's a detective, actually. And yes, it was a stroke of good luck."

The dinner was excellent. Cal's paupiettes were savory, the rice cooked to perfection, the presentation careful and artistic. Nena complimented him on his cooking, and he, in turn, praised her salad.

"The slices of cooked potato were a brilliant touch. I like a little novelty in a green salad."

She started to say that the leftover boiled potato had been rolling around in the bottom of her refrigerator for a week, but she stopped herself. Instead, she smiled and accepted the compliment.

After dessert—a mango sorbet with almond biscotti and decaf espresso—they cleared the table and spread out a highway map of Mexico.

"I think we should head for the central part of the country. That's where my relatives are," she said.

"Do we drive or fly?"

"Why not take the bus?" Nena replied.

"The *bus?*" Cal's eyebrows arched high over his sea blue eyes.

"Sure. First-class bus service in Mexico is far better than here in the States, it's a good way to see the countryside, and it's terrifically cheap. Driving in Mexico is a pretty terrifying experience."

"In all honesty, Nena, I don't know if I care to spend my precious vacation rolling down the road with the proletariat. You will forgive me, I hope."

She shrugged. "We could drive my truck, I suppose. It's a little risky taking a ten-year-old vehicle on a long, hard drive like that. Plus Toyota parts might be difficult to find in Mexico. Forget taking your Beamer down there. It wouldn't make it five inches past the border before it got stolen.

"Why can't we fly and rent a car?"

Nena hesitated. That meant the vacation would cost more than she could really afford. But she didn't want to tell Cal that, for fear he might cancel the trip altogether. Well, there were always those credit cards she never used.

"Sure," she said. "I suppose we could fly to Mexico City and rent a car there."

Poring over the map, they laid out a tentative itinerary.

"We can leave the day after Christmas, and fly via Dallas to

Mexico City, where we can spend a couple of days sightseeing," she said.

"Isn't Mexico City dangerously polluted?"

"Yes, but if there's a breeze, it's not so bad in the parts of town we'll be visiting. Besides, it's a fantastic place with world-class museums, cutting-edge architecture, pre-Columbian temples, great restaurants. I think you'll be impressed. We'll rent a car there and head for San Miguel de Allende."

"What's there?"

"It's a pretty little colonial town a few hours to the north-west of Mexico City, the darling of American visitors. Lots of historic charm, a pleasant spring-like climate, and it has a host of creature comforts like restaurants, coffee bars, shops, English language periodicals, and bookstores. The place where I usually stay has a small pool and good food, and we can walk everywhere. I think San Miguel would be a great way to introduce you to traditional Mexico. One of my favorite cousins, Pepe Herrera, lives there. He's the vice-rector of the Bellas Artes school and teaches metalsmithing."

"You're sure we shouldn't just head for a beach, like Acapulco?"

"Don't you want to see Mexico?" Nena asked. "Mexican beach resorts are like resorts anywhere—high-rise hotels, chain restaurants, phony architecture, high-priced everything, hardly any Mexicans, except for the help, and they're often understandably surly. Acapulco has grown into a big ugly city with more than a million people. I want to show you authentic *México*."

"Oh," Cal said. "I guess it'll be okay."

Nena was surprised at his reluctance to visit the Mexican interior. She'd chosen San Miguel as a safe, slightly sanitized version of her beloved *madre patria*.

"So where else are we going, Ms. Casey?"

"After a few days in San Miguel, we could go on to Guanajuato," she said, pointing the city out on the map. "I told you about it before. It's an old mining town, a university town, another Colonial-era jewel. It's a couple of hours' drive from San Miguel, through very pretty country. We could spend a day or two there. Then, before heading back to Mexico City, we can visit Dolores Hidalgo, where my mother's brother, Francisco Herrera—Tío Paco—is the chief of police."

"The chief of police?" Cal laughed. "I can just see him now—five two, potbellied, big droopy moustache, with his meaty paw outstretched to accept bribes—everything I've heard about Mexican cops."

Nena's temper flared. "Guess again, cowboy!" she retorted. "My Tío Paco is an Olympic medal winner. Rome, 1960, a silver in fencing. He's one of Mexico's star athletes. People still recognize him wherever he goes. He stays in terrific shape, frankly, far better than some people . . ." She poked Cal's soft belly. "And he's as honest as anyone I know. His family has a sizeable cattle ranch. I don't think he needs to put his hand in anybody's pocket. He likes being a cop, and he's an excellent one. In fact, last year, the Federal Law Enforcement Training Center in Marana, Arizona, invited him to give a lecture to American cops on border issues."

Cal put his arms up defensively. "Christ! I had no intention of offending you, dear. I'm sure your uncle is a decent fellow."

"You'd better believe it," Nena said. "And my aunt is a sweetheart. She comes from a family of famous potters. You're forewarned. Dolores Hidalgo is where we load up the car with pottery. For years, I've wanted to buy a set of the hand-painted dishes the town is famous for and my aunt will help me find the best work for a good price."

"By then, I'll be so good in Spanish, I'll be able to do the haggling for you," Cal said.

"You're serious about wanting me to teach you Spanish?"

"*Sí, señorita,*" Cal nodded. "I plan to take full advantage of your talents on this trip, I hope you know."

"You do, huh?" A little leer stole across Nena's face.

Cal blushed. "Um, I meant . . . your . . . linguistic skills. In fact, I think I should offer you some remuneration—like maybe I could pay for the rental car."

Nena bit her lip and looked very serious. Then she began to speak in an exaggerated Spanish accent. "Ooooh, Señor Banner, there are names for arrangements like that. I think about your yenerous offer, but first, I must tell you, I also plan to take advantage of your talents."

Cal threw an arm around Nena's shoulder, drew her close, and whispered in her ear. "Perhaps we could practice taking advantage of each other's talents now, señorita?"

＊　　＊　　＊　　＊　　＊

Later, as she lay beside him in the dark, her bare toes rubbing against his stockinged feet under the covers, a loneliness and a longing to be elsewhere suddenly came over Nena. She wanted to be in her own house, in her own bed, wearing her flannel granny gown, curled up beneath her feather quilt, sleeping to the soothing creak of the baseboard heaters. She missed the coyotes' evening concerts, and the purr of the orange ball of fur warming her feet at the end of her bed.

She propped her head up on her elbow and twirled a couple

of Cal's curly red chest hairs between her fingers. She knew he wasn't asleep yet. "Would you mind terribly if I went home?"

Cal stirred and opened one eye. "Now?"

She nodded.

"My dear, it's past midnight. Do you think it's safe for you to drive home by yourself at this hour?"

"I'll be fine, *corazón,*" she said, pecking his cheek and getting out of bed. "After all, this is my town."

She gathered her clothes from the bedroom floor and dressed quickly, knowing his eyes were on her. "Stay put, Cal. I'll let myself out." Leaning over him, she gave him a quick kiss and her hand lingered on his face. "Thanks for a marvelous dinner and a truly wonderful evening," she said, stroking his cheek. "I'll talk to you next week."

Cal crossed his arms behind his head on the pillow.

As Nena left his bedroom, she heard him mutter, "Who was that masked woman?"

17

The streets around the university were still bustling at one in the morning. But as Nena drove into the North Valley, traffic thinned until the roadways were nearly empty. While she waited in a well-illuminated intersection for a green light, she saw in her rear view mirror a large, dark-colored truck with oversized tires rapidly approaching, its powerful motor rumbling loudly over the rattling idle of her Toyota.

There was something ominous about the big truck and the aggressive way it was gaining on her that unnerved Nena. When the light changed to green, she floored the accelerator as the big pick-up swerved around her left side, missing her bumper by inches. Although the driver didn't look her way, he drew alongside and slowed to match her speed. Nena recognized him in the bright overhead lights of the next intersection—the frizzy dark hair, his gray beard, the jagged scar that ran down his right cheek.

For what seemed like hours, she drove cautiously north, her heart throbbing as the muscle truck drove alongside her, inches from her driver's side door, its engine grumbling. Thoroughly frightened, she stared straight ahead, her knuckles white as she clutched the steering wheel.

She felt her heart might explode from the tension, when the truck suddenly braked and squealed into a left-hand U-turn. Shocked, Nena turned to watch it speed south and away from her. She caught sight of an old-style blue and white police car a half-block behind her. Relieved, she filled her lungs with gulps of air and relaxed her death grip on the wheel.

As she drove over the Rio Grande on the Paseo del Norte freeway toward Corrales and home, she found herself frequently checking her rear-view mirror for any sign of the fat-tire pickup. Only the APD blue and white stayed in view, steadily maintaining a half-block distance. "Strange," she mused. "If my quirky tail-light is out again, or if the cop thinks I'm driving funny, wouldn't he have pulled me over by now? Maybe he's driving home, too. Otherwise, why would an Albuquerque cop be outside his jurisdiction in the middle of the night?"

As she slowed to make her turn into Casey Boulevard, the cop car zoomed past, continuing north on Corrales Road. In the dark, she couldn't see the driver. In fact, she wouldn't have been able to say if the cop was male or female, or in uniform.

Happy to be home, she parked by her back door, where Flaco sat on the GO AWAY mat, patiently waiting for her. Her house had never been more inviting.

18

Early Monday morning, when the dawn light cut through the blinds in Nena's bedroom, she awoke to find everything outside thickly coated with hoarfrost. The telephone wires on Casey Boulevard, the fence lines in the fields around her house, every branch and berry of the Russian olives, every single blade of grass was rimed with blue-tinged ice. Majestic white cottonwoods spread a matrix of alabaster branches against a brilliant cobalt-blue sky. Even the spider webs in the corners of her bedroom windows had been intricately articulated in lace-like ice, and the windowpanes were spangled with crystal fans. Overnight, Mother Nature had transformed the bare, dirt-brown New Mexico winter landscape into a pristine white world. Everything in sight sparkled in the new sunshine.

Nena dressed in her warmest jogging clothes and stepped outside. The air was cold enough to freeze her breath, and it burned the inside of her nose when she inhaled. Still, she found it exhilarating to be out in the enchanted landscape, the ice grass crunching loudly underfoot and the birds calling excitedly to one another from their perches in the white-veneered trees.

The dirt on the ditch path was a sharp-edged frosting of frozen mud. Because the footing was treacherous, Nena elected to walk rather than jog—all the better to soak in the morning's rare beauty. Before she knew it, she had reached her turn-around point. Off to her right, she spied a pair of coyotes trotting quickly through clumps of sage, their mottled gray and sand-colored fur a perfect camouflage in the frosted greens and browns of high-desert vegetation.

Suddenly, a frightened cottontail burst through the sage, zigzagging its way toward Nena. The coyotes caught sight of the rabbit and took out after it, bounding through the chaparral, their black-tipped tails straight out behind them like wind socks.

"Hey!" Nena called out loudly, waving her arms and running toward them. Startled, they hesitated, then tore off into the sagebrush, and quickly disappeared.

At the base of a chamisa bush, the rabbit huddled, trembling with fright, its large, red-violet eye intent on Nena. She stopped and watched as a wet patch spread out from under the terrified animal. "Oh, *conejito!*" she said softly. "I didn't mean to scare the pee out of you! Now, you'd better hide quickly, or those mean coyotes will have you for breakfast."

The rabbit blinked, wiggled its nose, and hopped off into the brush.

With a smile, Nena turned toward home.

*   *   *   *   *

She was standing at the stove, stirring oatmeal, when a knock came at the back door. There stood Luis with a newspaper under his arm. She waved him in. He stomped his work boots on the mat. "Guess you scared those coyotes good, *hermana!*" he laughed. "I bet they're still running!"

"Are you spying on me?"

"Nope," Luis said. "The paperboy missed my house this morning. I was driving over to the Frontier Mart for the *Journal* when I saw this crazy lady on the ditchbank waving her arms, chasing off a pair of coyotes that tore through the brush like their tails were on fire. Ay, Coyota! People are gonna talk!"

Nena laughed. "Oh, they were after this cute little cottontail and I didn't want them to murder it."

Luis shrugged. "It's their job, you know. Their bread and butter. Talk to my wife about cute little cottontails. The ones that won't leave her lettuce alone."

"Yeah, I know, I know."

"Hey, how was the flea market?"

"I had a pretty good day yesterday, and Saturday was terrific—my best day ever. I'm exhausted."

"Eee, that's not from work. That's from too much partyin.' I can tell. That gavacho . . ."

"Careful, I have a weapon."

"Oh? You're going to hit me with your spoon? Rosita says you told her you're going to Mexico with that guy. Are you really? Not that it's any of my business . . ."

"You're right. It's not any of your business! Yes, I am going to Mexico with . . . 'that guy,' as you call him. We're leaving the day after Christmas. Tony's going to feed Flaco for me while I'm gone."

Luis frowned. "He doesn't seem like your kinda guy, Nena. He's so . . ."

"So . . . what? White? Is that what you're trying to say? You haven't even met him!"

"No—although he does sound pretty white. You'd better not let him out in a frost like the one this morning. You'd never find him again."

Nena growled. "Actually, he's pink—not white."

"I don't have anything against him for that. Except from what you've told me, he's got to be kind of square."

"What? Because he doesn't drive a humongous pick-up and toss Coors cans out the window, and he doesn't go out in the mountains to murder large, dumb animals the way you and the other *vatos* do? And maybe because he's from back east and he's educated, you don't like him. I know that. But you know what? I like him. And I'm the one going out with him—not you!"

"Good thing. He's probably not my type."

Nena waggled the spoon in his face, and Luis backed up, laughing. "Chill, girl. You've made your point. You don't have to get violet . . ."

"You mean 'violent,' don't you?"

"No, I mean 'violet.' You're a little purple right now, *'mana*. Take it easy! "

Nena put the spoon down giggling.

"Are you bringing him to Christmas dinner at Mom's?"

"Are you kidding? That would be like feeding a tasty Christian to starving lions. Mom would start asking him how much the university pays him, and if he's a Catholic, and what we're going to name our children. You know how she is . . ."

Luis grinned broadly. "Uh huh. Chick-ennnn . . ."

"Yup. You called it. Chicken is exactly what I am. Hey, how come you're not out building dream homes today?"

"Rosita and I are doing year-end bookkeeping and the payroll. Seeing what kind of a Christmas bonus we can give the crew. If there's anything left over, if we have the *feria*, we're going Christmas shopping. And you?"

"Correcting exams. That's the day's order. I need to get my grades in."

"Give 'em all A's. Make it easy on yourself. By the way, have you seen this morning's paper?"

"No. They didn't deliver my paper today, either."

"There's an article on the front page about your student. The investigators are leaning more and more toward the crash being a suicide." He studied her quizzically, waiting for her reaction.

"Oooooh God, I have a terrible feeling about this!" Nena's good mood melted and her stomach began to twist in knots. "Hey, I talked to the man three or four hours before he died. Trust me, Luis, he was not suicidal. He was excited about getting married."

"That's what his fiancée says, too. Apparently, he had some rough patches in his life, like maybe he used to have a drug problem. In the past couple of years, though, he turned himself around. She's demanding an investigation, and so are his parents. His tanks had jet fuel in them, not aviation gas."

"Jet fuel?"

"That's what the paper says, although they also describe him as an experienced pilot who'd been flying since he was sixteen."

"Dammit." Nena stamped her foot. "Those DEA guys said something about fixing tanks, I know they did! This is awful! What do I do, Luis? His poor girlfriend! His family!"

"I'm telling you, Coyota, talk to Ruben. He'll know how to deal with this."

"Aw, shit. I don't know what I heard, I really don't. Maybe what those guys were saying had nothing at all to do with that plane crash."

"It's up to you. I can't tell you what to do."

Nena smiled faintly. "You're learning, 'mano."

"Just think how his girlfriend feels. She knows he didn't kill himself."

"So do I." She paused for a few moments. "I suppose I should tell you about another weird thing."

Luis took a deep breath and closed his eyes. After several

seconds he opened them. "Okay," he said, "I'm ready. Lay it on me."

"Well, there's this *hombre* who's been following me . . ." She told him about the black truck that shadowed her on the way home from Cal's, and the man in the Taurus pacing her as she jogged. "I think it's the same guy. He has a scar on his cheek like the *chota,* the cop I saw at customs."

"Christ, Nena! Why didn't you tell me this before now?"

"I mean I wasn't totally sure he was following me. I'm still not sure. Who's gonna believe this? It's too bizarre!"

"Hermana, get a grip. This is serious. I can and will help you, but you have to decide whether or not to go to the authorities, and the sooner the better."

19

"Merry Christmas! Feliz Navidad, everybody!" Nena called out to the clan of relatives that filled her mother's living room on Christmas day. Wending her way through the festive chaos of discarded wrapping paper, boxes and ribbon, she gave *abrazos* to everyone and distributed packages from the large shigra over her shoulder. "*¡Feliz Navidad! ¡Felices Pascuas!* Merry Christmas!"

"Eee, Tía Nena, is that your Santa Claus bag?" asked a little girl in a red velvet dress, pointing to Nena's colorful striped tote.

She nodded. "Yup. And I've got a present in here for you, Yoli." She brought out a soft parcel wrapped in bright-red Christmas foil. The little girl took the package and immediately ripped the paper off it in one stroke and tossed it aside.

"Oh, it's a little Indian doll," she said with disappointment in her voice.

"It's from Ecuador, m'hija. From way far off in South America."

"Don't they have Barbies over there?" Yoli asked.

"Maybe. But there are a bazillion Barbies. This doll is special. It's maybe the only one like it anywhere in the world. And I got it just for you, from the lady who made it."

The little girl smiled wanly. "I love my Barbies," she prattled. "Momma got me a Beach Barbie for Christmas. She has a bikini and flippers and a scooper tank!"

"Scuba tank, Yoli," Crucita said, coaching her daughter. "Now, say thank you to your Tia Nena . . . "

"Thank you, Tía Nena," the little girl parroted tonelessly. Then, tossing the doll on top of the crumpled wrapping paper, she went off to join a group of children clustered around a boy playing Nintendo by the Christmas tree.

"Well, maybe she'll appreciate it when she's older." Nena laughed.

Crucita shrugged. "Maybe."

The living room was filled with the din of grown-ups talking and laughing, while kids screamed and argued and giggled. In the background, the beeping of electronic games competed with Christmas music coming from a Spanish radio station and the sound of clanging pots and pans in the kitchen.

Luis appeared at Nena's elbow. "Can I get you a beer? Mom also has the rompope out, if you're up for disgusting sweet yellow goop that'll knock you on your can."

"Gee, what a salesman you are, Luis. I'll have a beer—if there's any real beer in the house. A Negra Modelo or a Dos Equis would be great."

"Coming right up—a Bud Light for the lady."

"You're incorrigible."

The doorbell rang. Several of the children ran to answer it.

"¡Mamá!" Yoli yelled above the noise. "It's a man with flowers!"

Crucita went to the door and accepted a huge pot of pink poinsettias from a deliveryman. She took a small envelope from the side of the plant and read it. "It's addressed to Mrs. Sebastian Casey. It's for Mom."

"¡Gramita!" Yoli shrieked as she ran through the living room into the kitchen. "Flowers! Somebody sent you flowers!"

Felipita Casey came into the living room wiping her hands on her apron. "Flowers? Who send them to me? Oh, they so pretty! *¡Nochebuenas!* Pink ones!"

Various family members gathered around Felipita and the large, foil-wrapped pot. Crucita handed the envelope to her mother.

"Who's it from, Gramita?" Yoli asked.

"I have no idea," Felipita replied as she pulled out a pair of reading glasses from her apron pocket, put them on, and opened the small envelope. 'Merry Christmas to Mrs. Sebastian Casey and all the family. Sincerely yours, Caldwell Oates Banner III,'" she read.

Everyone looked at Nena, who blushed.

"Oh, how nice of your young man, Azucena," Felipita said. "Such beautiful flowers he send me. Too bad he is not here with us for Christmas dinner."

Nena's color deepened.

Minutes later, the doorbell rang again. Once more, Yoli ran to open the door. Another deliveryman stood in the doorway, his face hidden behind a large bouquet of pink Peruvian lilies, tea roses, and asparagus ferns.

Crucita joined her daughter at the door, took the flowers from the man, and read the small envelope taped to the green waxed-tissue wrapping on the bouquet. "It's addressed to Doña Felipita Herrera de Casey *y toda la familia,*" she said.

"More flowers for you, Granma!" the little girl screeched.

Crucita gave her mother the flowers and the card.

Everyone in the room watched as Felipita opened the second envelope and read the enclosed note to herself. "Ay, that Ruben," she sighed. "He always was so considerate."

All eyes again turned to Nena.

She spun around and strode into the kitchen. "I'll find a vase, Mamá," she called out.

*   *   *   *   *

Sixteen people were seated at the table, including several non-family members whom Nena's mother called *"los huérfanos,"* the "orphans" who didn't have any place else to go for Christmas dinner. Luis carried in a beautifully bronzed turkey and set it down in front of Crucita's husband, Gilbert, who was seated at the foot of the table next to his mother, Angelina.

Felipita asked Luis to lead the grace. "And don't let's forget the ones who are not here, m'hijo. Your father, *qué en paz descanse,* your brother, Estéban, who never come home from that terrible Vietnam, Crucita's first baby, our *angelita . . .*"

"Do you want me to say grace? Or do you want to do it, Mom?" Luis said grinning.

"Oh, no, m'hijo. Is for you to say the grace. You are my oldest and the man of the family. My children never give me a priest or a nun. So it's for you to say the grace."

Nena, Crucita, and Luis exchanged glances, trying not to smile.

Felipita untied her apron and draped it over the back of a kitchen chair. She took her place next to her son.

Luis stood behind his chair. The rest of the guests sat down, took the hands of those to either side of them, and bowed their heads. "Let us thank the Lord for all his goodness and for this beautiful meal," he prayed. "We remember all those who aren't with us today, our beloved father Sebastián and our sadly missed brother, Steve. Crucita and Gilbert's baby. The homeless, those in prison, the many people in the world who are hungry and destitute." Luis paused and grinning ever so subtly, he added "And let us also think about special friends who can't be present today, like Nena's amigos who sent Mom the lovely flowers."

He looked down the table to where Nena sat. She shot him the evil eye.

When Luis finished saying grace, everyone except the smallest children made the sign of the cross and said *amén.*

Gilbert did his best at carving the large bird, but the pieces he cut were either skimpy slices or thick, clumsy slabs of meat. He served the children first, passing their plates to their mothers, who spooned more food onto them from steaming bowls in the center of the table: Spanish rice, *calabacitas,* stuffing, tamales, red chile sauce. By the time Gilbert had placed slices of turkey on the last adult's plate, the children had finished their servings and were clamoring like starving baby chicks for more food.

Gilbert groused. "Give me a break, chamacos! Jeez!" Pulling a handkerchief from his pocket, he daubed at the beads of sweat that dotted his forehead.

"Don't forget your father's plate, m'hijo." Gilbert's mother Angelina trilled in a tiny, bird-song voice. "He'll be home any minute from his job in Califas. *Ya mismo viene.* He's on his way."

"Where's Califas?" Tony whispered to Nena.

"It's California," she whispered back. "He left home forty years ago, and they never heard from him again."

"Oh," said Tony.

Yoli overheard and piped up. "Who never came home again, Tía Nena?"

"Shhhh, *niña!*" Felipita hissed.

There was an embarrassed pause in the conversation, but soon everyone was talking loudly again, over a maelstrom of activity. Plates, bowls of food, bottles of Pepsi and beer traveled up, down, and across the table as silverware clanged against china and glasses clinked.

"When are you and your friend leaving for México, Nena?" Crucita asked.

"Mañana."

"Now—which *amiga* you are going with?" Felipita asked.

Nena chewed her mouthful of calabacitas and glowered at Luis, who crossed his arms behind his head, leaned back in his chair, and delighted in watching his sister squirm.

Nena swallowed. "With a friend from the university, Mamita."

Luis grinned.

"In fact," she added. "Let's call Mexico from here this afternoon, so you can wish Tío Paco and his family a Feliz Navidad, and I can tell him we're coming. I didn't have his telephone number at home."

"She's going with that gavacho, Mom," Crucita said. "The guy with the fifty-dollar name who sent you the poinsettias."

Felipita regarded Nena in stunned surprise as Nena looked daggers at her sister. "We talk about this later, hija," Felipita said tersely, dropping her napkin beside her plate and standing up. "Now, who wants *café* with the Christmas pie?"

After dinner, Nena didn't say a word to her sister as they worked side-by-side clearing the table, washing dishes, and storing the leftovers. But when Crucita went into the back bedroom to fetch her family's coats, Nena followed her. She stood in the doorway, blocking her sister's exit, her hands on her hips. "Why did you do that?"

"Do what?" Crucita asked, her arms heavy with coats and scarves, her face a mask of innocence.

"Tell Mom I'm going to Mexico with Cal. Knowing full well it would upset her."

"She would have found out anyway, María Azucena. Tío Paco's family is going to notice you're traveling with a man, you know."

"I'm thirty-two years old, and it's my life. What's it to you, *cabrona?*"

"I'm leaving. I don't have to put up with you calling me names. *¿Quién te crees?* Who do you think you are anyway? Move aside. *I* have to go to work tomorrow."

"That's it—*celos.* You're jealous because I'm going to Mexico and you're not. Boy, this is tiresome."

Luis came out of the bathroom down the hall and called out cheerfully "No bloodletting, niñas! It's Christmas!"

Nena stepped aside as Crucita swept past her with her armload of coats, her nose high in the air.

Luis put his hands on Nena's shoulders, grinning broadly. "Gee, aren't you sorry you didn't invite Caldwell Oates Banner III to our family's lovely Christmas dinner?"

20

That night, Nena packed for her trip as a blizzard swept through New Mexico. With the wind whistling through the trees, hurling snow pellets at her house, it was difficult to imagine she would soon be in warm weather and that she needed to pack filmy cottons, not heavy winter clothes. "Let's see. Skirts, blouses, pants, a swimming suit . . . my most presentable underwear . . ." She mused as she put things in her suitcase. "Now, what am I forgetting? Pay bills, set out the cat food where Tony can find it, water my house plants, turn down the heat . . ."

She put her plane ticket and passport into her purse and added several pieces of outgoing mail. Surveying her packed bags, Nena reflected on one more piece of unfinished business and sighed heavily. "Now for the most important task of all, the one I've already put off too long. I have to tell Luis I've made up my mind to go to the police about the conversation I overheard at customs, and damn the consequences. It's the right thing to do—the only thing. For Chuck LaCour, for his *novia,* for his family, and for me."

She had reached her decision in the early hours of Christmas morning after tossing in her covers half the night, and she planned to talk to Luis about it after dinner at her mother's. With everyone around, that was impossible. Now, with a blizzard beating outside, she wasn't inspired to walk down the street to his house. She peered out the window at the snow blowing sideways. "Brrrr! No way I'm going out in that!" Calling Luis would be the easy and comfortable thing to do, still she hesitated. "Are my phone calls really private?" she asked herself. Herself answered: "Like Luis says, you never know."

"Well, I'll e-mail him," she decided. "Maybe that's safer than a phone call." She booted up her computer and logged on to AOL.

When she checked her e-mail before going to bed, she found a reply from Luis. "You've made the right decision, Coyota. I knew you would. While you're gone, I'll find out the best and safest route to take, who you should talk to. I'll help you get through this. Now—wipe the whole sorry mess out of your mind, forget about it completely, and have a blast in Mexico with your gavacho. Please give my *saludos* to the entire Herrera family! And don't forget to bring Mamita a jar of *cajeta*. Love, Luis."

21

"How do you say airplane in Spanish?" Cal asked, as their plane waited to take off from Albuquerque International.

"*Avión.* If you really want me to teach you Spanish on this trip, first you have to listen to a lecture on my philosophy of language learning."

Cal groaned.

"*Es muy importante,*" Nena said, clutching his hand. Maybe her little sermon would take her mind off her nervousness about the trip, and the realization that she was about to fly over the spot where Carlos crashed less than two weeks ago. While their plane moved slowly toward the head of the line of airplanes awaiting their turn, she began her discourse. "Unlike other types of learning, foreign language study requires the student to trust that what the teacher is telling him is correct. That she knows what she's talking about and is giving the student the proper information. The last thing a student should ask the teacher is why."

"Why?" Cal asked.

"Oh, boy. You already broke rule number one." Nena laughed. "Because there's often no rhyme or reason to a language. It's just the way it is. There are norms and there is logic to its structure, of course. However a lot of it is irregular and no language always follows its own rules. The teacher is really an informant, the one who knows the path and can lead those down it who aren't in the know. The student needs to suspend judgment about the correctness or fallibility of what he is being told—his critical thinking—and simply absorb the information the teacher gives him."

Cal looked perplexed, wrinkling his forehead in deep grooves of concentration.

She continued. "Think about how babies learn language. They imitate. They accept the sounds and patterns they hear, and parrot them back. Though gradually, they come to understand the language innately and can anticipate patterns of speech. We all know how fast children up to, say, their mid teens pick up other languages. It's because they're sponges. If you want to learn a new language quickly and well, you have to become as passive as a baby about it. Can you do that?"

Cal smiled, but didn't answer.

"In my experience, people with a scientific bent often have difficulties learning a new language,"

"Why's that?"

"Because they've been trained in analytical thinking, they learn by asking why, and they're used to hard and fast rules."

"So who's good at languages?" Cal asked.

"People who are musical, people who mimic well, people who are non-rigid in their thinking, and women tend to do better."

"Why women?"

"I find that adult men hate to appear silly. When you're new to a language, you're going to make mistakes. You're going to act and sound stupid, you won't know the answers, and your ability to function in the language will necessarily be elementary and infantile. A lot of men can't handle that. They don't like to look bad. A woman's need to look good is overtaken by her desire to communicate, however primitive the level. We're used to not being in power, I guess."

"Very interesting. But as my teacher you are in power —correct?"

"As the person who knows the language—and you don't—I'm in absolute power. I'm the dictator and you're the flunky. You vill do as I say!"

"Sí, señorita. Now that we've gotten that out of the way, give me the basics, like how do I greet people?"

"¡Ay, profesor! No, I tell you what's important. I design the course—not you. This is my show, meester. *¿Comprende?*

Cal studied the ceiling as the plane whooshed down the runway and pointed its nose into the sky. "Sí, señorita," he sighed.

"Sí, profesora," Nena corrected.

*　　*　　*　　*　　*

After a full day of travel, Nena and Cal arrived in Mexico City as the sunset was tinting the capital's sky a smoky orange. They checked into the María Cristina, a small hotel that catered to Mexican business travelers and veteran American *turistas* like Nena. Located a block from the Paseo de la Reforma, one of the capital's main thoroughfares, its rooms were spare, functional, and clean. Nena turned her charm on the desk clerk in flawless Spanish, earning them one of the better rooms, a suite overlooking the small garden at the back of the hotel.

Once they were settled into their room, she smiled at Cal and wrapped her arms around his waist. *"Qué dices—¿una cerveza?"*

Cal rubbed his chin in consternation.

Nena gave him a squeeze. *"¿Una Tecate? ¿Una Negra Modelo? ¿Una Dos Equis? Cerveza. Mmmmmm. ¿O quizás una margarita?"*

Cal brightened. "Ahhh, sí, profesora. ¡Margarita!"

Nena draped her wool ruana over her shoulders and grabbed her purse and the room key. *"Vamos, mi amor,"* she said, leading Cal by the hand.

22

Nena first noticed the young mustachioed man in cowboy garb the next morning as she jogged to the corner kiosk to buy a newspaper. After breakfast, when she and Cal strode toward the Reforma on their way to the Anthropology Museum, he fell in behind them. Nena spun around and glared at him. He halted in front of a store window as a bright green Volkswagen taxi slowed to turn into the next side street. Nena flagged down the driver, grabbed Cal's hand, and pulled him into the back seat. As they sped off, she saw the cowboy quickly walk back toward the hotel, waving at a man parked in a black Bronco. That afternoon, while she and Cal were having a cappuccino in the Zona Rosa, he reappeared, pacing back and forth in front of their café.

As Nena and Cal made the rounds of tourist spots over the next couple of days, she saw other similarly-dressed men tailing them. She didn't think they were thieves or pickpockets. They looked too clean, too innocent, and too out of their element in the urbane capital. Their provincial clothes alone—snap button shirts, steel-tipped lizard-skin cowboy boots, and gray Stetsons pulled low over their ears in the chill winter winds—set them apart from the *chilangos,* the Mexico City natives. Nena guessed they were *norteños*—northerners—from one side or the other of the U.S.-Mexico border, where nineteenth-century German ranchers and local Indian women had produced a tall, slim, black-haired, dark-skinned, green-eyed *raza.*

Nena decided not to point out the surveillance to Cal. He

was already on edge, being in a third-world city for the first time in his life. Plus he didn't know the language, couldn't read the signs, and understood little of what was going on around him. She didn't want to add to his unease. And she didn't think he'd believe her. Nevertheless, being followed was very upsetting, and she was furious that their privacy was being invaded.

When a norteño photographed them coming out of the Franz Mayer Museum, she decided she had to speak up. "That guy just took our picture," she said, gesturing toward a man in a tan canvas barn coat who was quickly walking away down the street.

"So what?" Cal said. "Can we go back to the hotel now? My stomach's bothering me. I've had enough touristing for the day."

Nena decided to drop the subject, at least for the moment.

*   *   *   *   *

The afternoon before they left for San Miguel, yet one more snoopy cowboy showed up, standing at her elbow, leaning over her as she filled out paperwork at Budget Rent-A-Car for a Volkswagen to pick up the next morning. She faced him abruptly. "*¿Qué quieres?*" she demanded angrily.

Startled, he walked out without answering and sat on a bench in the park on the other side of the street, twirling his cowboy hat in his hands, watching the door of the car-rental agency.

As she left the office, she saw him talking to a short, blond, jug-eared gringo in glasses. The two of them glanced her way before turning their backs on her. Nena got only a glimpse of the gringo. There were a lot of round-headed, glasses-wearing blond men in the world, even in Mexico City. But she'd seen this particular one before, in the customs office in Albuquerque the day she overheard a certain conversation.

Her hands shaking and every nerve on edge, she walked slowly back to the María Cristina, trying to gain control of herself. Should she tell Cal about the men following them? If she did, she'd have to tell him about the incident at the Albuquerque airport and her suspicions about the accident. Cal Banner had his good points, and he could be charming and solicitous. But unlike Luis or, Nena thought ruefully, Ruben, his masculinity was of the blustery sort. He didn't have the take-charge, protective, and dependable sort of machismo that would help her deal with this bizarre situation.

Cal was sitting at the desk in their room, reading the *Mexico City News* when Nena let herself in.

"*¡Hola, profesora!*" he called to her. "*¿Qué tal?* Oh dear, you seem unduly preoccupied. What's the matter?"

She sat down on the bed. "There's something weird going on, Cal, and I have to tell you about it."

He put down the newspaper and listened pensively as she recounted the events back in Albuquerque—the two men she overheard at the airport who seemed to be talking about fixing a plane's tanks, her former student's plane crash, the newspaper story suggesting his tanks might have had the wrong fuel in them, the break-in at her house, the U.S. West truck, the man watching her jog down the ditch, the muscle truck on her way home from his house. She told him about the norteños following them around Mexico City. "A minute ago, outside the Budget office, one of them was talking to the short, blond DEA agent I saw at the customs office in Albuquerque."

Nena could see that Cal was skeptical. His brow was creased, his eyebrows heavy, his eyes narrowed. "I know it sounds loopy," she said. "That's why I didn't say anything to you before now."

He leaned back in his chair and studied her carefully. "Are

you sure your imagination isn't in overdrive, dear? You're not quite certain what you heard the men talking about at customs. You say nothing was missing from your house. And now you think people are following you. Why would anyone be following us? I mean, we *are* in a primitive country and it's completely understandable that we're both a little nervous because of that."

"Primitive?" Nena frowned, taken aback. "You may be on edge, but I'm not. Mexico City is a second home to me, Cal. I'm Mexican on my mom's side, as you may recall. I spent two years here as a student. I've been coming to this hotel since I was a little kid."

Cal stiffened, bit his lower lip, and rubbed the tip of his long flared nose. "Nena, you can't be telling me you think this man, this customs officer…"

"DEA, Cal. They're not from customs."

He ignored her. ". . . this American cop would actually follow you all the way down here, do you? That's ridiculous!"

Although she felt herself on the verge of tears, she was damned if she was going to cry. "Yes, it's preposterous, and it's absurd. I guess you don't believe me, but goddammit, it's true!"

Cal sighed. "I think you're tired, dear. Maybe we've been overdoing the tourism, traipsing hither and yon from morning to midnight. The physical activity, the spicy food, the altitude— it's a lot to contend with. Moreover, I think you're still worn out after last semester. You overexert yourself. You've got more than a full plate with your teaching, your studies, and your little flea market enterprise. You're probably under a strain from the holidays, with that big family of yours. I'm sorry that I didn't realize that until now. Maybe this trip is too much for you."

Nena reddened. "I'm not over-tired. I'm not under strain. I was enjoying myself immensely until this lunacy began. And I am absolutely not imagining this, Cal. Let's just drop it! It was a mistake to bring it up. Forget I said anything to you at all. I know—let's go have dinner. The real reality is that I've been dying for *mole verde* all day."

"I was sort of thinking I'd like a hamburger."

Nena gasped. "Never order a burger outside the U.S.. It's one of my cardinal rules of travel."

"Why?"

"Instead of ground beef, it might be ground burro!" she teased.

Cal scoffed. "I would think that in a good, respectable restaurant like Burger King one could be assured of the quality of the meat, even in Mexico."

"I suppose you're right. They'd at least skin the critter first."

23

After a night of fitful sleep, Nena rose early. Cal stirred and squinted at her with half-open, unfocused eyes. "I'm going to go get the car," she said. "Don't be in a hurry to get up."

He grunted his assent, rolled over, and went back to sleep.

Nena hummed a little tune to herself as she strolled toward the Budget office on the far side of the Reforma. She was happily anticipating the drive to San Miguel and being out of Mexico City's smog and bustle.

Beams of light cut through the early morning haze, illuminating the dew that glistened on the leaves of the trees and shrubs. In front of stores, apartment buildings, and office towers, maids were out washing the sidewalks, swishing foamy water with their brooms, while in every side street, parking attendants slapped rags on the shiny flanks of cars that were triple-parked across driveways, sidewalks, and medians.

Although the reek of exhaust fumes was omnipresent, there was a freshness to the late December morning, a lingering memory of the Valley of Mexico's better days, when its high, thin air was pure and fragrant with the scent of flowers, eucalyptus, and pine trees. Unfortunately, the city's frenetic, jumbled concentration of too many people and vehicles, shabby buildings, and abused vegetation was now almost always enveloped in a foul soup of smog. Nena still revered the capital. With its rich past: Indian, Spanish, African, even Chinese; and its exciting, uniquely Mexican present, Mexico City reminded her of a *grande dame* down on her luck.

Nearing the Reforma, she stopped to admire a row of elegant, hand-hammered silver bowls in a shop window. At once, she saw the reflection of a norteño standing behind her. When he noticed her glaring at him, he feigned interest in the window of the art gallery next door.

Furious, Nena spun on her heel and strode up to him. "*¡Lárgate! ¿Me oyes? ¡Lárgate, y déjame en paz!*" she yelled at him fiercely, telling him in no uncertain terms to beat it and leave her alone.

The man's eyes widened and his jaw dropped. Obediently, he quickly walked away, his boot heels rapidly tapping the pavement.

On the other side of the street, a young maid in a pink uniform stopped whisking her broom around the soapy sidewalk to gape at Nena in astonishment. Nena caught her eye and smiled nervously before continuing on her way toward the Reforma, wondering if perhaps she hadn't just given a poor, innocent campesino the shock of his life. Had he really been following her? Was the surveillance all in her head? Was Cal right that she was imagining things?

As she stood on the edge of the tree-shaded boulevard waiting to cross, she told herself to get a grip. "Relax and enjoy the trip, Nena. Don't spoil things. There's nothing weird going on. It's all in your head, *chica!*"

Forty minutes later, she walked back into the hotel room and dropped a set of car keys on the bureau next to Cal's *Beginning Spanish* book. He stood at the sink, wiping the remains of shaving foam off his jaw and neck with a towel.

"*¿Quieres desayuno?*" she asked. "Care for breakfast? You need to fortify yourself for the wildest ride of your life."

His eyes widened. "Is it that bad?"

She nodded. "I promise you, Mexico City is the most terrifying driving experience you'll ever have."

He folded the towel and laid it beside the sink. "I can hardly wait," he said.

24

"Oh my God—watch out, Nena!" Cal yelped. "Jesus! Did you see that? That car drove right across six lanes of traffic and you just missed it by inches! Oh, Christ! There's another one—on the left! Look out!" He slapped the sides of his head with both hands.

"Shut up, Cal, darling," she said. She swerved to miss a deep pothole and whisked the Volkswagen around the rear fender of an old truck wobbling down the road on a bent axle, farting clouds of black smoke from a crooked tail pipe fastened to its bumper with baling wire.

"I'm only trying to be helpful," he said testily.

"You're not being helpful. You're messing up my concentration, yelling at me constantly. Trust me—the best thing for you to do is keep quiet."

His jaw snapped shut, and he crossed his arms over his chest. "This is madness, sheer madness," he muttered. "These people are fucking maniacs!"

"I warned you. This is why I suggested taking the bus. Close your eyes, corazón. Maybe that will help."

He did his best to be quiet, but as cars zoomed around their Volkswagen, or braked inches in front of or behind them, he winced and ducked and moaned and swore. Nena held the steering wheel firmly, rarely blinking, her head swiveling in constant surveillance as she made sharp stops and quick accelerations to avoid collisions. For more than an hour they wove in and out of the swirling, chaotic stream of traffic that flowed north out of Mexico City, past endless stretches of grim cement buildings and shabby shopping centers, pastel-painted apartment towers flying flags of flapping laundry, shacks made out of packing crates and sheets of corrugated metal, heaps of garbage, and scrawny, scavenging dogs.

At the northern edge of the city, Nena suggested they stop for a break. "Now that you've seen unfortunate and ugly aspects of Mexico, let me show you something extraordinarily lovely."

"That would be a welcome change," Cal said.

In the middle of a grimy industrial sector, she left the highway and followed signs to the town of Tepotzotlán. As they neared the city center, she pulled off the road and stopped in a residential area.

"Now what?" asked Cal.

"We peel all the stickers off this car that say it's a rental, and put everything we don't carry with us into the trunk. Not even a map or book should be showing. ¿Comprendes? Take everything valuable with you—your passport, your money, your camera."

"Whatever you say, profesora," Cal said.

Nena drove to the town's main plaza and parked. Because it was mid-morning on a weekday, the square was quiet. Tepotzotlán's restaurants, shops, and *artesanía* vendors still awaited the busloads of tourists that descended on the town every day. A little old man in a khaki jumpsuit trotted up as Nena locked the car. She gave him fifty pesos, generous payment for keeping an eye on the vehicle, but declined his offer to polish it with his filthy red rag. They shouldered their cameras and tote bags, and walked toward the magnificent high-baroque church. Glancing back to memorize their parking spot, Nena noticed a small red sedan parking behind their car. She watched as a young Latino couple got out. They, too, dropped coins in the old man's outstretched hand.

Cal and Nena stood on the broad, cobblestoned plaza in front of the church amid a swirl of foraging pigeons to examine its single-towered white stone facade. The bas-relief carved *estípite* columns were twined with plants, animals, saints, and chubby angels.

Nena grinned at Cal. "Whaddaya think?"

"It's riotous," he exclaimed. "Emblematic, perhaps, of this mad country."

"But it's a controlled riot. See how all the details are worked out? The symmetry? Wait 'til you see the inside. This is a tabula rasa by comparison to the main altar *retablo.*"

At the entrance to the Museum of Viceregal Art, housed in a 17th century *convento,* they bought tickets and stepped into a quiet cloister of barrel-vaulted ceilings and courtyard gardens that had been converted into one of the country's premier museums. Room after room in the old monastery had been adorned with religious paintings, sculptures, and decorative arts from the Viceregal period, Mexico's gilded age, when it was the center of Spain's wealthy province of *Nueva España.*

As they strolled through the galleries, Nena could tell Cal was impressed.

"I found the Franz Mayer Museum interesting. But this is quite a scene," he said.

"The Franz Mayer rivals this museum, for sure. Part of their collections, especially the Talavera pottery and the furniture, are better. Yet I think this place retains a sense of the splendor of the era, its exuberance and sensuality. Next, I'm going to show you a real riot. Ready?"

As they entered the nave of the San Francisco Javier church adjacent to the convento, Cal's eyes widened in amazement. On all sides, floor to ceiling, the church vibrated with color and movement in a dazzling display of ornamentation. On the main altar, intricately carved columns, polychromed and gilded, framed a pantheon of *santos,* each in its own niche.

"It makes me dizzy," he said. "I guess this is what art historians mean by *horror vacui.*"

"Oh, you dour Protestants," Nena said. "You just don't know how to have a good time! The Jesuits were out to convert the Indians with the promise of heaven and all its riches, and this church is one of their masterpieces. It's no wonder the Pope was pressured into expelling them from the Americas in 1757. They were making anything done by rival orders look wimpy by comparison. How could anyone compete with this?"

He continually muttered in amazement as they explored the church, taking in the rich display and high-baroque details. When he seemed to have seen enough, Nena asked. "¿Quieres café?"

"Oh, sí. Café. ¡Magnífico!" he responded with enthusiasm.

To one side of the church, a patio had been converted into an outdoor restaurant, its pillars and archways hung with swags of bougainvillea in all shades of pink, red, and orange. Cal and Nena collapsed into chairs at an empty table and ordered coffee and mineral water. She reached over and held his hand. "Feel a little better?"

He nodded. "The museum was splendid. Still I have to tell you, dear, you're driving like a maniac. I can't believe it! You're going to get us killed. You never drive like that in the States."

She clasped her hands together on the granite-topped table. "You have to drive like they do here or you will get killed.

It's another culture, another language, and another way of driving."

"It's insane!"

"You have to trust me that I know what I'm doing, Cal. Or, do you want to drive?"

"Hell, no!"

"I know it doesn't look like I'm being careful, but I am. I'm doing my best. I don't want to die any sooner than you do."

A young woman in a crisp yellow blouse and skirt brought a laden tray and set down cups of steaming black coffee, bottles of mineral water, and glasses in front of them. Cal took a paper napkin from the dispenser and wiped the rims of his cup and glass. Nena watched him in wonder.

"What?" Cal said. "I am merely being extra cautious, dear. Don't make a federal case out of it."

To her right, Nena saw a man at the next table aim a camera in her direction and snap a picture. She recognized the couple from the red sedan. The man forwarded his film and set the camera down with a subtle smile. His female companion sat slack jawed, puffing a cigarette. She stared at Nena with sleepy eyes that were slightly crossed.

"We just had our picture taken again, Banner," she said quietly, pouring cream into her coffee from a little blue and white pitcher.

Cal looked up from the edge of his cup.

"The man next to us—to your left," she said, reaching for the sugar bowl.

He glanced at the couple, who ignored him. "He wasn't taking our picture, Nena," Cal scolded. "What is the matter with you?"

"Oh, silly me. I guess he was photographing the entrance to the john. Or perhaps the garbage can?"

He peered behind Nena. She was right. The only thing beyond them was the restaurant's least scenic corner, which featured an overflowing trash bin and the door to the restroom. "You're trying my patience, dear," he scowled.

"And you're trying mine," she replied, sipping her coffee.

25

On the highway north to Querétaro, traffic thinned to two loosely-defined lanes on each side of the median. Slow, chugging trucks and busses meandered all over the road, while small cars and SUVs whizzed around their VW like meteors.

"Christ—don't these people know how to stay in a lane?" Cal groused.

"Honey, you have to understand. Mexican drivers consider traffic lane stripes *sugerencias*—suggestions—not hard and fast rules," she said breaking into laughter.

"It's not funny," Cal said. "It's whacko, and it's very, very dangerous!"

Half an hour past Querétaro, Nena turned west onto a well-maintained, two-lane asphalt road that meandered through rolling countryside. The sun was out, and the skies had cleared to a milky blue streaked with wisps of thin, white clouds. Pink, ivory, and lavender wildflowers dotted the hillsides. "We're almost there," she said.

Cal continued to gaze emptily at the landscape.

As they neared San Miguel de Allende, traffic became dense and slow-moving. The road dipped down a sharp incline and narrowed. Nena guided the Volkswagen cautiously through a tumultuous maze of vehicles. Children, dogs, and chickens strayed into the road, as did shoppers clustered around busy roadside stands that spilled out onto the pavement.

The car rumbled down cobblestone streets past colonial

churches, small, tree-shaded parks, and handsome adobe build-ings stuccoed in a palette of bright colors, their roofs rippled with red clay tiles, their windows barred in wrought iron. Nena made a series of turns onto side streets and drove up a steep driveway into a courtyard surrounded by an arcade. The hotel walls were painted in varying shades of deep blue and turquoise, with touches of *rosa mexicana* and red around the frames of doors and windows. Under a bougainvillea-draped portico, she parked the VW in front of a sign that said *oficina*. A chamber-maid walked out the office door, her arms piled high with folded sheets and towels.

"*¡Bienvenidos!*" she said pleasantly.

"*¡Gracias!*" Nena said. She nudged Cal, who was half-asleep. "*Llegamos.* This is home, the Posada San Pascual."

"Finally," he muttered.

*　　*　　*　　*　　*

After they checked into a large corner room, they sat down to lunch in the glass-enclosed restaurant at the end of a veranda.

"At long last, a welcome relief from Mexican food," Cal mum-bled as he read over the menu. Suddenly, he burst out laughing. "I love this: 'smashed potatoes!' 'meatlove!' Oh, and this, this is priceless: 'fried mind!' What the hell is that?"

Nena read the Spanish side of the menu. "'*Sesos fritos.*' You don't want to order that, Cal. It's brains."

"I don't need to. I've already got fried mind."

When the elderly Indian waitress came to take their orders, Cal asked Nena to order for him. "I'll have the smashed potatoes and meatlove," he tittered.

"Aren't you going to try out your Spanish? She'll understand you," Nena said as the waitress stood by patiently.

"No way, José," Cal said.

Nena ordered for him, and for herself, she asked for *enchiladas suizas*. Neither of them spoke much during lunch. They ate and went back to their room. "I'm going to walk over to the Bellas Artes school to see if I can find my cousin, Pepe," she said. "Do you want to come?"

"I think I'll have a siesta. I need to recover from fried mind," Cal said. He lay down on the bed and turned his back to her.

26

As Nena walked the narrow sidewalks in the direction of the art school, she considered her traveling companion. She was seeing a Cal Banner she hadn't seen back in Albuquerque, and she didn't much like him. He was stuffy, unadventurous, snobbish. He slept a lot, getting up late, going to bed early, taking long naps every afternoon. He didn't want to practice speaking Spanish because he said it strained his voice.

"My throat is bothering me," he continually grumbled. "Probably from breathing all this chemical gunk. I certainly hope Mexico City's foul air isn't causing my vocal chords irreparable damage."

"The air here is almost as bad as it is in Los Angeles, wouldn't you say?" Nena said pointedly, knowing Cal got his doctorate at UCLA.

He ignored her. "My voice is very important to me, Nena. After all, I'm a professor, and my profession depends on my speaking ability."

Then there were places he wouldn't go because he had heard they were unsafe—the markets, which were her favorite haunts, and Chapultepec Park.

Nena scoffed. "I have never heard of anyone being accosted in Chapultepec. That's ridiculous, Cal. Roosevelt Park in Albuquerque is far more dangerous. People come from all over the world to enjoy the bosque. It has centuries old trees, lakes, and pathways. The walk up to the *Castillo,* the Castle, is especially lovely. It feels like you're back in the 1860s, during Maximilian's brief reign, and Empress Carlota's carriage is going to roll past you at any moment. Their palace is now the National Museum of History. You're a historian. I should think you'd find the place interesting."

He wasn't swayed. "I'd rather have a snooze. Frankly, there's no history in this hemisphere of any interest to me."

Nena was flabbergasted, but she said nothing. She went to Chapultepec by herself and enjoyed a delightful afternoon in the museum.

Cal also griped endlessly about the food, describing the most bland dishes as "spicy." They hadn't been in the country two hours before he began complaining of indigestion, although they hadn't eaten anything but tortilla chips with their drinks in the hotel courtyard. He never wanted to be more than five minutes from a bathroom, which severely restricted their sightseeing. Nena took them to the best and safest restaurants she knew, and she suggested the mildest things on the menu for him. It didn't matter.

Mexico City had fabulous restaurants: cozy little places that featured regional dishes: *veracruzano, oaxaqueño, poblano, norteño.* Argentine-style steakhouses with plate-sized *churrascos* and herby *chimichurri* sauce. Spanish restaurants with savory paellas. And a host of neighborhood cafés that provided reasonably-priced, international dishes and Mexican favorites. Nena wanted to explore them all, but Cal protested. He absolutely refused to go into her very favorite restaurant, Tacos al Caminero, a hole-in-the-wall eatery near the American Embassy that featured grilled meats, fresh corn tortillas, and a variety of salsas; he didn't relent until he saw a group of Americans in pinstripe suits descend from a limo and walk in the door. Even then, he wouldn't try the salsas, though he reluctantly admitted that the roll-your-own tacos were "tolerable."

The Spanish lessons were a *fracaso*. Cal was the most recalcitrant student Nena had ever encountered in her eight years of teaching Spanish. He not only questioned her methodology, he questioned the material she was trying to teach him. He didn't seem to believe her that it was *"el mapa"*—not *"la mapa."* And *"el programa"*—not *"la programa."* He was reluctant to try out his Spanish, even to say "por favor" or "gracias." He seemed to have a block toward the language. She wondered if it wasn't a reflection of his negative attitude toward the country and its people.

Now that she'd spent four days in his company, Cal struck her as an unadventurous, sluggish, and boring hypochondriac. Maybe he was also a racist. He was certainly ethnocentric. He didn't have a single good thing to say about Mexico or the Mexicans. The country was filthy and dilapidated. Primitive. Inferior. He preferred Cleveland's museums to Mexico's. Spanish Colonial furniture was clunky and crude compared to Federal. The painting was third-rate, the religious sculpture gory and idolatrous. The desk clerk fumbled his English. The taxi drivers were all thieves. The English language newspaper didn't have his favorite cartoons. The bottled water wasn't trustworthy. In spite of Nena's good-natured and heroic efforts to show him the best of a city she knew well and loved, Cal whined continually about everything.

He had also lost interest in sex. He was too tired, or his stomach was bothering him, or he wanted to read his *Time* magazine, which, he pointed out to Nena, was on cheap paper and way thinner than the U.S. edition.

Telling him about the surveillance was a huge mistake. He said she was delusional. He even made fun of her. That morning at breakfast, he shoved the vase of flowers over the table to her. "Don't you want to see if there's a microphone in here?" he cackled.

Being with Cal was worse than being alone. He was a drag.

27

"*¡Prima!*" Nena's cousin Pepe called out when she walked into the courtyard of the old monastery that housed the art school.

"*¡Primo!*" She laughed back.

They engulfed each other in exuberant hugs beside a splashing fountain.

"I am sooooo happy to see you, Pepe!" she said. After three days in Mexico City with Cal, twenty million strangers, and the shadowy norteño escorts, she was truly relieved to see a friendly, familiar face. Her lively, dark-haired cousin was barely an inch taller than Nena, a smaller and more tanned version of her brother, Luis. He was a handsome man with powerful shoulders and arms, his warm brown face lit up by shiny, coffee-bean eyes and a huge, disarming smile that tipped up the corners of his sleek black mustache.

"Papi phoned me that you were coming. Julia and the kids are dying to see you. Where's your *novio*? We can't wait to meet him. Is this the one, Nena?"

She sighed. "Oh, well, Pepe. He's not really my novio. Especially not after this trip. He's back at the hotel. Getting his beauty sleep."

"Ay, prima. We're going to have to find you a Mexican boyfriend. That's what you need. But for now—*¿Qué dices? ¿Un cafécito?* I have a half-hour before my faculty meeting."

They adjourned to the cheerful, student cafeteria tucked into a corner of the colonial building. Over a steamy cup of *café con leche,* Nena told him about the trip thus far. She considered telling him about the norteños, but there was really no time. If she told Pepe, the whole family would know it in minutes. He would call his father, Tío Paco would immediately ride to the rescue of his favorite niece, and her vacation with Cal would be over. Besides, maybe Cal was right—maybe she was simply over-reacting.

Before Pepe went off to his appointment, they made plans for a festive lunch with his family at his house the next day.

Nena walked back to the hotel. She knocked gently on the door, and getting no answer, she let herself into the room. Cal groaned and rolled over, rubbing his eyes.

"Have a good nap?" she asked.

"This bed is terrible," he moaned. "God, it's like sleeping on marshmallows."

"Do you want me to see about another room?"

"No. I'll just take an extra sleeping pill tonight."

"Be careful with those things, Cal. They're addictive."

"Don't nag," he snapped. "I hate to be nagged."

Nena let the subject drop. "Can I interest you in a stroll? The light is gorgeous out there. The town is at its loveliest at twilight."

"Is it sundown already? What happened to the afternoon?"

"It appears you whiled it away on that Beautyrest, dear," Nena said.

"Ah, yes." He yawned. "Well, let's go hunt up a couple of drinks. Any good watering holes in this burg? I have a thirst that needs slaking."

"That's another thing," Nena realized. "He drinks too much."

28

At dusk, San Miguel's narrow sidewalks were alive with children playing, meandering dogs, people doing last minute shopping before the stores closed. Clusters of neighbors and friends laughed and chatted and waved at cars passing by. In a completely different rhythm, American tourists made their way around and through the throng, looking either slightly lost or intent on being elsewhere fast. Their sandals slapped the pavement noisily as they hurried along with their heads down.

Nena took Cal's hand. "Let's go sit in the plaza for a bit. It's wild at this hour."

In the town's busy main square, she steered him to a park bench where a heavy-set Indian woman with two little wide-eyed girls in braids smiled and made room for them. Cal wiped the bench with a handkerchief before he sat down. "What's all the racket?" he asked.

"I think they're grackles. They converge on this place every day at sunset."

Hundreds of birds shook the trees in the plaza with their exuberant chirping and fluttering, taking off in sudden bursts, then landing again, the whir of their comings and goings sounding like waves crashing on a beach. The park was filled with people every bit as busy and as noisy as the birds. They strolled beneath the trees and stopped to talk with friends. Teenage girls giggled and flirted with gawky teenage boys. Elderly couples walked slowly arm-in-arm. Young parents pushed strollers.

Women trundled shopping bags full of groceries. At the edge of the park, taxi drivers put their feet up on the bumpers of their battered cars and bummed cigarettes off each other while waiting for fares. Shoeshine boys whisked rags over the tops of their patrons' shoes and collected tips. Traffic slowly rounded the square in a symphony of honking horns, perforated mufflers, and squealing brakes.

"I don't know when I've experienced such a racket. Is there a special event today?" Cal asked.

"It's almost New Year's Eve." Nena said. "But the plaza's like this every night. Isn't it amazing?"

He rolled his eyes. "My God."

Nena continued. "It used to be that the girls would walk around the square clock-wise, while the boys would walk around the perimeter counter clock-wise, in sort of a courting ritual, with Mom or Dad or Granny sharp-eyed to it all from a park bench. It's a charming and very old custom. You may see that here."

*　　*　　*　　*　　*

As they sat on the bench taking in the twilight bustle, an American in a black shirt and jeans bought a bag of popcorn from a street vendor. Sauntering around the periphery of the plaza, tossing popcorn into his mouth, he searched the crowd for Nena and Cal. When he saw them sitting on a bench next to an Indian family, he looked for a spot from which he could keep an eye on them.

Things weren't quite working out the way he and his partner had envisioned. Their original plan had been to follow the woman and her boyfriend into Mexico alone. There, with the help of their contacts among Mexico's federal police force, they could easily arrange to have the pair nailed on set-up drug charges. Back in Albuquerque, they could push their *jefe* for a search warrant to officially raid the woman's house in Corrales, where they'd turn up her cute little Band-Aid tin of dope. And find more significant drugs they would plant on her property. If María Azucena Herrera-Casey were facing drug charges in Mexico and in the U.S., nobody would believe her story about what she heard at the customs office. Or, failing that, maybe they could work out a deal with the broad to have all the charges dropped if she agreed to keep her mouth shut.

However events had taken a different turn. Their jefe insisted they take a group of new DEA agents with them on their trip to Mexico to follow the woman they had told him was part of a major drug smuggling ring. The kids were dim-witted and green—a half-dozen norteños recruited from the Texas border area, an ugly chick from Taos, and a swishy fag from Nicaragua. But to the veteran agent's surprise, things actually seemed to be working out. In fact, the assignment was turning into a plum. The trainees made the operation appear more official and on the level. They did most of the grunt work, following Casey and her boyfriend around Mexico City and on their drive through the countryside, while the man and his partner engaged in a little extracurricular business with their Mexican associates. Now here they all were in a nice little provincial town. It was disappointing that the targets hadn't gravitated toward the nightclub scene, where it would be easier to arrange a set-up. Nevertheless he was confident there'd be a way of pulling off a drug bust. They had a lot riding on the success of this gig. A whole lot.

*   *   *   *   *

Nena watched a vendor help an excited little girl in a lacy pink dress select a balloon from the bright colored assortment he held by their strings, while several toddlers chased pigeons, to the amusement of their parents. Suddenly, she saw a bearded man in a black shirt and jeans sitting on a bench near the balloon vendor leer at her. The sight of his beard, the thick thatch of black hair, and more than anything, the scar that ran down his right cheek from the corner of his eye made her stop breathing. He showed her a tight-lipped smile, tossed a popcorn kernel high in the air, caught it in his small, sharp teeth, and chewed it slowly before swallowing.

She shuddered.

"A friend of yours?" Cal asked.

"Who?"

"The Cisco Kid over there." Cal said pointing in the man's direction.

The man got up off the park bench, balled up the popcorn bag, tossed it into a trash barrel, hiked up his jeans, and strolled off.

Nena took a deep breath. "Let's go get a drink," she said.

*   *   *   *   *

The next day, Cal refused to go to Pepe and Julia's house for lunch. "My stomach is already making rumbling noises. I'd better not push my luck with more of this exotic food. You go on without me. Think I'll rest up."

Nena was annoyed.

"Besides," Cal added. "Spanish hurts my head. The language is as melodic to the ear as a jackhammer, and it's no fun not knowing what people are saying about you."

"What makes you think they would be talking about you? Besides, both of them speak flawless English. Pepe studied at the Art Institute in Chicago, and Julia did her pre-med studies at Northwestern. They met in Chicago, in fact."

"I'm just not up for it. Please thank them for wishing to include me."

"This is really rude of you, Cal. They're both very busy people. Pepe runs the art school and Julia has a full-time medical practice. They're going out of their way to be hospitable to us. The least you could do is show up. I promise you, a visit to their place is well worth it. They live in a beautiful 18th-century hacienda that's been in Julia's family for generations. They raise chickens and ducks and horses, and have three adorable kids. Their housekeeper is a renowned cook. Some of her recipes are in Diana Kennedy's cookbooks. I should think you'd be thrilled to have what is likely to be a superb meal in beautiful surroundings with delightful, interesting people."

"Really, Nena. I appreciate your wanting to include me in your family gathering. I'm simply not in the mood. Let's not make an issue of this."

Nena left the room closing the door firmly behind her.

*　　*　　*　　*　　*

Cal was happy to see her go. The last thing he wanted to do was spend an afternoon with her relatives and feel pressured to be polite and eat whatever they served him. Nena was annoying him with her insistence on Mexican food, although she knew it didn't sit well with him. She rarely gave him any choice about restaurants, or what they might do or see. Frankly, she was running him ragged, dragging him through one museum after another even knowing he wasn't the least bit interested in Mexican art or artifacts, especially not that horrific Aztec stuff. He would retch if he had to see another one of those gaudy churches with the bloody statuary she seemed to be so in love with. And why had they risked life and limb to travel to this dumpy little town? He didn't find it the least bit quaint. The streets weren't even paved, and they were in the middle of nowhere. What if he had a medical emergency?

Back in Albuquerque, Nena seemed lovely, intriguing and sensuous, a radical change from the brittle, lock-jawed, horse-faced girls he'd grown up with, two of whom he'd married, with disastrous consequences. But here his brown-skinned sylph was proving to be too much for him. She was too pushy, too foreign, too independent. At the very least, he regretted not insisting on a vacation in Acapulco or another first-class, cosmopolitan beach resort. In fact, he was sorry he'd made the trip at all.

He turned on his side, clutched the mushy pillow, and tried to sleep.

29

Nena was right. Julia and Pepe's housekeeper did prepare a special lunch, a delicately-flavored squash blossom soup followed by home-raised chicken braised in wine and almonds, crusty *bolillo* rolls, and a salad made from greens grown in the hacienda garden. Dessert was an orange flan served with Nena's favorite, *café de olla*—cinnamon-flavored coffee prepared in an earthenware jar and served in matching cups.

After lunch, they adjourned to a verandah shaded by a grape-arbor overlooking the orchard and vegetable garden. As they sipped tiny glasses of Kahlua and cream, Nena again apologized for Cal's absence. "He missed a lovely lunch. I don't think I've ever had a more wonderful meal anywhere," she said.

"Would you like me to make a house call?" Julia asked.

"Thank you, no. I don't think he has anything serious. He's a bit of a hypochondriac, to tell you the truth, and he sleeps half the day."

"Do I sense that things aren't going so well between you two?" Pepe asked. "I don't mean to pry, Nena . . ."

She laughed. "Oh, I don't mind. Well, let me put it this way. You find out a lot about a person by traveling with him. Things you hadn't noticed before."

"That's why I'm happy I lived with Pepe for almost a year before we came back to Mexico and got married," Julia said. "At least I knew what I was getting into. Can you believe it—he puts his sugar on his corn flakes before he pours the milk on them!"

"Ay, amor, you're telling all my secrets. Can you believe it, Nena? She puts the sugar on after she's poured the milk. How absurd! I married her anyway, fool that I am."

*   *   *   *   *

Nena returned to the hotel late in the afternoon, to find Cal sitting on a bench outside their room reading a year-old *People* magazine and drinking a beer.

"I see you're feeling better," she said.

"I had a nice nap after lunch, and I'm feeling quite chipper, actually. How was your visit?"

Nena described the menu in glowing detail. "You missed a fabulous meal."

"I had spaghetti and meatballs here. It wasn't all that great. I did meet a nice young couple over lunch, however. The people who sat next to us in the café at Totopo . . . however you say it . . . the town with that screaming baroque church. They're from Texas—El Paso—and they're staying here, too. The young man is quite interested in history. In fact, he saw my article about Celtic settlements along the Danube in *History Today* last year, although I don't think he actually read it.

"By the way, he says he didn't take your photograph while we were having coffee at that church. You were mistaken. He was photographing a butterfly. I invited them to join us for dinner."

Nena put her purse down. "I don't think I'll be interested in eating tonight. I'm still full from lunch."

"Surely you can come along for the company, then."

"We'll see."

*   *   *   *   *

Nena decided to stay at the hotel and read instead of joining Cal and his new pals for pizza. She truly wasn't hungry, and she relished some time alone. When he got back late that evening, she was propped up in bed with her book, a Paco Ignacio Taibo III *novela*. Cal was more than a little drunk and seemed to be feeling frisky. She watched as he pulled his shirt and sweater over his head and tossed them into a corner of the room in a pathetic attempt to imitate a male stripper. With a bump and grind on unsteady legs, he undid his belt buckle and zipper and dropped his pants and shorts, nearly tripping as he struggled out of them.

"I'd like to invite you to take advantage of me," he slurred as he stood swaying alongside the bed, naked save for his black socks.

Nena closed her book, keeping a finger on the page she'd been reading. "'Not tonight, darling. I have a headache.'"

Cal sat down hard on the bed. As he bent over to peel his socks off, he nearly slipped off the edge and had to grab hold of the thick nubby bedspread to steady himself. "You know those kids? The ones I thought were so nice? They wanted me to snort cocaine with them. Can you believe that? Who woulda guessed they were coke-heads?"

Nena wasn't surprised. In fact, she could have predicted it.

His swirling eyes searched out hers in the dim light of their room. "No nookie, huh?"

"Sorry, cowboy." She inserted a piece of Kleenex in her book to mark the page, and switched off the bedside lamp. "The campfire's gone out."

30

The following afternoon, while Cal took his siesta after lunch, Nena walked over to the Bellas Artes school. She needed to talk to her cousin in private.

They met in his office. Pepe leaned against the edge of his desk, his head down as he sipped a Pepsi and listened intently to what Nena had to tell him about the conversation, the plane crash, the break-in, and the strangeness back at home; about the norteños in Mexico City; about the couple who had photographed her and offered Cal coke; and about the DEA guys who seemed to show up wherever they went.

When she finished, he grimaced. "Pretty heavy, prima. I think you should talk to Papi. Forget going to Guanajuato. Go directly to Dolores Hidalgo. Do not pass Go; do not collect two hundred pesos. Maybe I should drive you there myself. You might be in serious danger."

"Why, Pepe?"

"Because they're chotas, Nena, that's why. You may well have serious goods on them—specifically, murder. Who knows how far they'll go to protect themselves? You Americans are naive about bad cops. We *mexicanos* are not. We know what they're capable of, especially if they think you're a threat to them. Look, Nena, from what you've told me, both of the guys you overheard in Albuquerque are here. In Mexico. That's not a coincidence. Something's up. And if your phone at home is tapped, they could have read your e-mail to Luis and know you plan to go to the authorities when you get back to the states."

"Isn't e-mail safer than a phone call?"

"Not exactly, prima. Your internet connection uses the phone lines, and these guys have all the techno-toys."

"I didn't think of that. Ay, Pepe, I'm so confused! I don't know for sure that my phone is tapped. I don't know if I'm being followed here in Mexico. Or if I'm getting paranoid. I don't know if any of this is real. Maybe it's all a coincidence. Maybe I'm seeing things that aren't there."

"Trust yourself, Nena. I know you. You're not one to imagine things. Does your friend know what's going on?"

"I tried to tell him, and he just blew me off. Said I was over-tired and delusional."

"Some friend he is! Dump the guy and go straight to my parents' house in Dolores Hidalgo."

"No, primo, I'm not ready to write him off. I think he's overwhelmed. He's never been anyplace like this before. Part of me still hopes the relationship is salvageable."

"María Azucena Herrera-Casey, you are an incurable optimist! You're in danger, prima! And it doesn't sound like Cal is any help to you whatsoever."

"Maybe he'll snap out of whatever's ailing him and revert to his charming self."

"Yeah, sure. Well, if you insist on staying with him, I have an idea. A great New Year's Eve might cheer you both up. The celebration on the plaza tonight is terrific—music, fireworks, a castillo. We never miss it. Go have a good dinner and a bucket of margaritas, then join us on the plaza. We'll save you space on a bench on the north side facing the *Parroquia*. Bring the boyfriend. I have to meet this dude and check him out. See why my favorite cousin's so stuck on him that she's willing to risk her neck."

✳   ✳   ✳   ✳   ✳

Nena let herself into the darkened hotel room. "Arise ye sleeping demons!" she called out to the lump on Cal's side of the bed.

"Whatever for?" a sleepy voice responded.

"It's New Year's Eve!"

"Is it even dark yet, Nena?"

"No, but it'll be night soon enough. Let's go out and play!"

"Let's not and say we did."

"Aww, c'mon, Cal. We can check out the shops, hunt up a good restaurant, maybe get a steak, wash it down with a few margaritas, watch the fireworks—you know, have a wild night out!"

Cal sat up and rubbed his eyes. "A wild night in this two-horse hamlet?"

31

They wandered through stores that featured punched-tin frames and lanterns, glassware, textiles, toys, and other things made by local craftsmen. In a shop that specialized in leather, Cal tried on a chocolate-brown, glove-leather vest. It fit him perfectly, and the stitching was impeccable.

"I like it, but I'm not sure I should buy it," he said hesitantly.

"Live it up!" Nena said. "Be daring! Spend money!"

"Is this a good price?" he whispered.

"It's forty dollars, Cal. A vest like that would easily cost you two hundred in the States, wouldn't it?"

"Yes, but shouldn't I haggle a little, just on principle."

"Be my guest."

"You mean you won't bargain for me?"

"No, I won't. They speak English here, you know."

The saleswoman was polite when Cal offered her fifteen dollars. "I'm sorry. Our prices are fixed. But if you'd like to buy the vest, I'll throw in a leather key holder."

Cal started to walk out the door.

"Where are you going?" Nena asked.

He came back and under his breath he said, "Aren't I supposed to make like I'm walking away from the deal?"

"¡Ay!" Nena said. "She told you their prices are fixed. Go on and buy it, Cal! It looks great on you, the price is more than fair, and I know you want it."

"Okay, okay." He paid for the vest and pocketed the key holder.

*　　*　　*　　*　　*

The evening had barely descended over San Miguel when the fireworks started. One after another, whizzing *cohetes* shot into the sky with whistling screams before detonating noisily. As they walked the streets arm in arm, Cal winced at each loud bang.

"Jesus! Is this the start of World War III?"

Nena laughed. "Wait until midnight. I'll bet it gets really deafening then."

"I can hardly wait," Cal said.

On a side street, they found a steak house and were lucky enough to get a table on the balcony. They sipped margaritas and enjoyed a clear view of the Plaza Principal, already filling with spectators. The Parroquia, the church of St. Michael the Archangel, presided over the square like a pink-turreted guardian. Dramatic lighting enhanced the details of its many rose-colored towers and pinnacles.

"That church is hilarious!" Cal said. "Look at those whacky pink-sugar spires. What would you call that architectural style—wedding-cake Gothic?"

Nena laughed. "Or perhaps cotton candy Gaudí? The Parroquia has always reminded me of Sleeping Beauty's castle at Disneyland. I like it a lot. It's fanciful, but graceful and pretty in its own way."

"Graceful? Pretty?" Cal scrunched his face in disbelief, leaned over, and surprised Nena with a kiss. "Happy New Year, darling."

"*Feliz Año Nuevo* to you, too," Nena said. Cal seemed more relaxed for a change, like he was almost enjoying himself. Maybe her optimism was well-founded after all. Or maybe the swimming pool-sized margaritas could account for the improvement in their mood.

After a leisurely dinner, Nena and Cal joined the campesinos, townspeople, foreign residents, and tourists—chilangos and Americans alike—converging on the *Jardín* from all directions. In the plaza's gazebo, mariachis played festive music. Their deep bass guitars, blaring trumpets, violins, and melodious male voices rebounded from the buildings surrounding the square and competed with small *conjuntos* of guitar-playing musicians strolling through the crowds.

"What cacophony!" Cal said, covering his ears. "One of these bands would be bad enough, but there must be a dozen different ones. God, I've never heard such sour notes!"

"Oh, lighten up, Cal. This is a fiesta—not a night at the Berlin Philharmonic."

The fence in front of the Parroquia was decked out with fireworks displaying profiles of Mexican historical figures—Father Hidalgo, Benito Juárez, Emiliano Zapata.

"What's that bizarre wooden scaffolding in front of the church?" Cal asked. "Is the Inquisition going to burn a few heretics tonight?"

"It's a castillo, a castle. The wheels are fireworks, and there are rockets attached to it, too. It must take weeks to make one of those—and seconds to blow it up."

"They're going to light that thing on fire? Here, in the middle of all these people?"

"Sure," Nena said. "I hope your insurance policy is paid up."

They elbowed their way through the thick, boisterous mass of people and found Pepe, Julia, and their three children sitting on one of the benches by the bandstand facing the Parroquia.

"¡Hola, prima!" Pepe called out.

Nena introduced Cal to him, the children, and Julia. The children gravely shook his hand, then ran off to watch the mariachis and play on the gazebo steps.

Moments later, the couple Cal had befriended the day before appeared out of nowhere.

"Hola, María and Nelson!" Cal said cheerfully. "What a pleasant surprise." He introduced them to Nena and her family, whose names he had already forgotten.

Nena was instantly on guard. She didn't like the couple showing up wherever they went, and she didn't want them intruding.

Nelson produced a camera. "Let's take pictures to have souvenirs of this happy occasion and Nena's lovely family," he said cheerfully. He began to set up a shot while Maria herded the children back to their parents.

Nena stepped between the camera and her family. "Sorry! Their agents don't allow unauthorized photos! The studio is very specific about that."

Cal and Julia gaped at her in wonder. Immediately, Pepe caught on. He walked up to Nelson and stood very close to him. "It's in our contract, you see. Only union photographers can take our picture." His smile had a hint of menace in it.

María and Nelson exchanged looks. He pocketed the camera. Cal was speechless.

Pepe hopped up on the bench. "Let's stand up here so the kids can see over people's heads. It's getting close to midnight." He held out a hand to Julia, then to Nena, then to Cal and helped them up. "Sorry," he said to Maria and Nelson. "There's not enough room for you."

Sensing that they were being dismissed, the couple melted into the crowd.

"What the fuck was that all about?" Cal muttered to Nena.

She didn't answer. Instead, she whispered to Pepe: "Those are the two I told you about. They've been tailing us since Tepotzotlán, they're staying at our hotel, and last night, they offered Cal cocaine."

"¡Jesucristo! I didn't like their looks, and I didn't appreciate the camera thing one little bit. Thanks for stopping them." In a low voice, he told Julia what Nena said. She nodded pensively.

Pepe and Julia clutched their two youngest children in their arms, and Nena hoisted the eldest child to her shoulders. As the multitude waited for the church bells to ring in the New Year, fireworks shot into the sky, bursting into noisy showers of color as spectators oohed and ahhhhed. Like meteors, cohetes streaked heavenward in bright flashes. Strings of firecrackers rat-tat-tatted like machinegun fire, smoke rising from them until the air was thick with the smell of gunpowder. As midnight approached, an electric current of anticipation surged through the plaza. Voices became louder and more animated. Children jumped up and down and squirmed with excitement. When the clock struck twelve, the Jardín exploded. The Parroquia's bells rang out loudly, competing with church bells from all over San Miguel. Rockets shot off into the sky in all directions, their debris raining down on the crowd. While fireworks lit up the night in cascades of jewel colors, barrages of firecrackers sounded from all corners. The wheels on the castillo spun madly, whirring and screaming in dizzying swirls of color and light. The noise was ear-splitting.

"¡Feliz Año Nuevo! Happy New Year!" Revelers shouted to each other above the din, kissing and hugging and dancing through the showers of sparks.

Shots rang out.

Cal yelled into Nena's ear "Was that gunfire?"

"Probably. Don't people in Newport shoot off guns on New Year's?"

"They certainly do not!"

"Well, they do here. Don't worry. They're probably blanks. Yahoo! Happy New Year!" She jumped up and down on the bench.

"I'm getting out of here," Cal said angrily. "This is insanity. I don't care to be hit by some drunken *pistolero's* stray shot." He jumped down and thrust his way through the crowd.

"A sudden bout of turista?" Pepe asked Nena.

"No," she replied. "I told you he was no fun."

*   *   *   *   *

The fireworks and explosions went on for another half hour, until people began to leave the plaza. The children were tired and the youngest fell asleep on Pepe's shoulder. "We're going to head home," he said.

"Thank you so much for inviting us. I'm sorry Cal was such an *aguafiestas*. But I enjoyed myself immensely! It was the most spectacular New Year's Eve ever! ¡Feliz Año Nuevo!"

As she hugged Pepe and Julia, Nena saw two men standing by the gazebo watching them: the scarred man in black, and the stocky man with blond hair and glasses. "The chotas are here," she whispered to Pepe. "The two gringos smoking cheroots over by the gazebo."

The men saw Pepe look toward them and quickly disappeared.

Pepe frowned. "Rough customers, Nena. I don't like this at all. We'll walk you to your hotel."

She protested. "I can get home by myself. I'll be fine."

They wouldn't hear of it.

32

The next afternoon, Cal and Nena checked out of the hotel. As they were loading their luggage into the VW for the drive to Guanajuato, Pepe appeared, carrying a small shopping bag. He shook Cal's hand.

"Are you feeling better today?" Pepe asked.

"Oh, yes, thank you. I was just a little unnerved by all that bedlam."

"Can I see you alone for a second?" Pepe asked Nena.

The cousins found a bench in the hotel garden while Cal finished packing the car. Pepe handed Nena the shopping bag. "I spoke to Papi last night on the telephone and told him about those American cops tailing you. We both think you should have this, at least until you get to Dolores Hidalgo."

Nena peered into the bag. "Oh, my God—a *cuete!* Take it back, Pepe. I'm not going to carry a gun in Mexico!"

"It's registered to Papi. He loaned it to me a while ago when I had to put down one of our old horses. It was his idea for you to have it. If anyone catches you with it, he can get you out of trouble. We both think you need to be able to defend yourself. Papi's planning on escorting you back to Mexico City."

Nena took a deep breath. "What kind is it?"

"It's a Smith & Wesson .38 special. It's clean and loaded and there are extra rounds in the bag. Have you ever used a .38?"

She nodded. "I hate guns, but my old boyfriend is a cop. He convinced me I needed to know how to shoot one."

"Ruben? What happened there, prima? I liked him. You guys were good together."

"It's a long story. I don't know if I should take this thing, Pepe. Guns scare me."

"Well, those guys scare me. I'm sure you won't need it, Nena. But at least you'll have protection if you do."

"Oh, alright. Thank you. I'd better get going now. I don't want to be on that road after dark. Please give my love to Julia and the niños."

"I will. *Qué Dios te cuide,* prima. Have a safe journey."

After Pepe left, Nena carefully tucked a scarf into the top of the shopping bag and set it on the floor of the Volkswagen behind the driver's seat.

"What's that?" Cal asked.

"Oh, it's a tool Pepe wants me to take back to his dad," she said.

Minutes later, they were on the way to Guanajuato, an hour and a half drive from San Miguel.

*   *   *   *   *

Their VW gallantly climbed up and down the road running through mountainous and mostly vacant countryside.

"So where are you taking me now, Madame Tour Guide?" Cal asked.

"Guanajuato. It's an old mining town. In its heyday, its mines produced about a fifth of the silver in the world. By the late 18th century, the mines were mostly played out, although mining still goes on. The city has a university, it's the state capital, and it's still a wealthy and influential town. In the early 1800s, Guanajuato was a hotbed of anti-Spanish sentiment, and important battles for Mexican independence took place there. And it's Diego Rivera's birthplace."

"How interesting," Cal mumbled from the passenger seat where he slouched against his door, absently watching the pine forest pass by the car windows in a green blur.

Like the day's weather, Nena's mood was sunny, and she was looking forward to visiting one of her favorite cities. She wasn't going to let Cal's lack of enthusiasm spoil things. Humming to herself, she negotiated the winding road with ease. Now and then she carefully passed a slow-moving, rickety farm truck laden with produce, livestock, or rough-sawn lumber. For the most part, however, there was little traffic. Passenger cars were rare, although as she rounded a sharp curve, she caught sight of a red sedan and a black SUV that had been a mile or so behind her since San Miguel.

As they approached Guanajuato, Nena said, "I have to warn you. We're going get lost at least twice before we find our hotel. The city's in a deep ravine, and it's a confusing labyrinth of streets that were once mining tunnels and burro paths." She made a few loops through the middle of town searching in vain for the Posada del Minero.

"Why the hell don't they mark the streets better?" Cal groused.

"That would take all the fun out of it!" she said cheerily. "Ah, Señor Banner, your infinite patience is rewarded. Here we are!" She parked in the lot behind a rambling, old-fashioned hotel that fronted the main square, the Jardín de la Unión. "*¡Servido, Señor!*"

"Let me guess," Cal said. "That means cocktail hour—right?" Nena sighed. "Well, why not."

33

A melon-colored dusk fell over the plaza, where a noisy chorus of birds and throngs of people had congregated. Cal and Nena settled into chairs on the hotel terrace facing the park and ordered margaritas. She wasn't at all surprised when moments later, María and Nelson descended on their table like a pair of pigeons.

"May we join you?" Nelson asked. Without waiting for a reply, they sat down.

"What a marvelous coincidence!" Cal said. "I didn't know you were heading this way."

María pulled a pack of cigarettes out of her purse. "I hope you don't mind if I smoke," she said, lit up, and blew a cloud of smoke in Nena's direction.

Nena did mind. Even the diluted dose of smoke stung her eyes, and she hated breathing in its acrid odor. But Cal didn't object, so she didn't either, not wanting to give an inch of satisfaction to this annoying woman. She took a sip of her margarita, licked the salt off her upper lip, and sat back in her chair with her arms folded.

"Is so nice to see you again, Nena," Nelson said. "You remember us? From the New Year's Eve? I am Nelson, and my friend, she is María."

"I remember," Nena said in a flat tone. To herself she said: "This is one coincidence too many. They're deliberately shadowing us. What are they after? That business with the cocaine was serious and scary. Why doesn't Cal understand how dangerous it is in Mexico to be around anyone carrying drugs?"

Nelson summoned a waiter and ordered whiskies, then began to chat with Cal. She noted that in English he had a heavy accent and a slight lisp. In Spanish, he swallowed his esses and ran his words together. His manner of speaking, together with his African-Indian-Mediterranean looks, suggested to Nena that he was Central American—Honduran or Nicaraguan. He was younger than María. They didn't often communicate with each other, either verbally or non-verbally, and in terms of personality, they were opposites. He was outgoing, talkative, and slightly effeminate, gesturing elegantly as he talked. María, by contrast, was hard and sullen. Nena doubted they were a real couple. They were partners in some shady deal Nena wanted no part of.

María caught Nena studying them. She narrowed her eyes in a display of thinly-veiled hostility and began to pick pieces of tobacco off her tongue.

To Nena, the woman had the tough looks and watchful wariness of a street fighter. Her long, sharp fingernails painted the color of arterial blood were especially menacing. She was nobody Nena wanted to tangle with. Yet Nena wouldn't be intimidated by her, either. María's wavy, coal-black hair and light-brown skin, her high cheekbones peppered with a few freckles, and eyes with an Indian cast to them, led Nena to guess that she was from New Mexico or Southern Colorado. She was either a cop or a criminal or both.

Maria was like a wary, nervous bird. She chain smoked and sipped her glass of whiskey, setting her drink down hard on the glass-topped table. She ordered a second glass of Scotch with mineral water, no ice, from the waiter in a self-conscious, fumbling, and flawed American-accented Spanglish. Nena almost sneered. Ordinarily, as a conscientious Spanish teacher, she'd never make fun of anyone's lame efforts to speak the language. But this situation wasn't ordinary. This was war—or at least a pitched battle. Nelson and Maria's invasion of their privacy, especially their intrusion into the New Year's celebration with Pepe and his family, unleashed an anger that took Nena by surprise, an aggression that was growing less subtle by the minute. If Cal would only back her up, she'd call a halt to the niceties and demand to know why the couple was following them.

But he blithely nattered on, oblivious to the wordless war between the two women. He enjoyed the couple's attention, easily slipping into his customary professorial role as if the three of them were spending a few moments together after class in the student union: the wise, jovial professor indulging solicitous students with a bit of his precious time and wisdom. Nelson fawned over Cal, calling him "Doctor" Banner, quizzing him about his research and writing projects.

Cal lapped it up.

Nena wanted to barf. Instead, she ordered another margarita in her facile, unaccented Mexican Spanish, chatted a bit with the waiter, and grinned smugly at María.

Cal and Nelson's conversation turned to San Miguel.

"So many tourists!" Cal complained. "The place is positively overrun with Americans!"

Nena groaned to herself. "This is an American tourist's favorite complaint, stupid, boring, myopic, and pointless," she thought. "A form of verbal self-abuse. Most Americans never want to go anywhere that hasn't been given the gringo stamp of approval. Monocultural guys like Cal only feel comfortable where there are plenty of English speakers, then they get all bent out of shape when there are too many of themselves." She wanted to break in and stand up for San Miguel as still being a real place, authentically Mexican in spite of the turistas, but she didn't want to participate in the conversation.

As the others gabbed on, she sipped her margarita quietly and shifted her attention to the fascinating whirlwind of activities in the Jardín, just beyond the wrought iron fence that separated the café from the public garden. The bustle reminded her of San Miguel's plaza at dusk except this park had a more urbane character, a distinctive *fin de siècle* quality, a twilight scene painted by Monet, with Guanajuato's handsome opera house in the background.

Nena was especially hoping to spot an *estudiantina. Tunas,* as they were popularly known, were bands of costumed, medieval-style, strolling troubadours from the university, who met in the plaza to begin their evening rounds. Music was one of Guanajuato's celebrated charms, and tuna ballads, with their lyrical harmonies, period instruments, and smooth male voices, were one of Nena's favorite musical forms.

Lights came on in the darkening plaza.

"I know," Nelson said, "Let's all go have a hamburger together at this terrific restaurant I hear about."

Nena begged off. "Go on ahead if you like, Cal. I'm bushed from the drive." She much preferred an evening with Paco Ignacio Taibo III and dinner on her own to one with the Weirdo Crashing Bores and a mystery-meat burger.

The three rose from the table to leave. "Just say no to worry, Nena," Nelson said, patting her arm. "We take good care of Doctor Banner."

"I'm sure you will," she replied. As Cal leaned over to give her a peck on the cheek, she whispered in his ear. "Keep your nose clean, cowboy. I'd hate to have to visit you in a Mexican jail."

He scowled at her. His face flushed in anger, he strode away with his new friends.

34

Hours later, Cal's fumbling at the door to their room woke Nena out of a deep sleep. She recognized his tuneless rendition of an old Beach Boys song as he stabbed at the lock with his room key. Finally, she got up and let him in. Not surprisingly, he was drunk. And there was a funny smell to him besides the stale bar odors of cigarettes and booze.

"I learned a new word in eshpañol!" he proudly announced, stumbling toward the bed.

"Uh, huh," Nena said. And what word is that?"

"¡Mota!" Cal said triumphantly.

Nena was incredulous. "You can't mean to tell me that you smoked dope with those people! How could you do anything so stupid? Stupid, stupid, stupid! Jesus H. Christ, Banner. Don't you have a few brains, drunk or not?"

"Don't be such a prig, Miz Herrera-Casey. You remind me of my last wife. She was such a prigging prig. Or was it the one before? Can't keep 'em straight. One of 'em, anyway. I haven't had a toke in a million years. It was great dope. Great mota! Mooooo-ta," he bellowed.

"Shhhh!" Nena said. "The whole hotel is going to hear you." Exasperated, she helped him undress and sat down on the bed.

Cal stood swaying in front of her, naked and grinning, his eyes glazed and unfocused. He lifted his floppy pink dick and wagged it in her face. "How about a little head?"

She curled her lip. "Not only do I have a headache, I think I might throw up."

"You don't know what fun is," Cal said. He clambered into bed, and in minutes, he was fast asleep, snoring loudly and snuffling like an old bear. When she was certain that he was out, Nena picked up his clothes from the floor and carefully went through his pockets. She felt a twinge of shame that was soon overcome by her self-preservation. If Cal had any dope on him, she had to get rid of it immediately. The last thing either of them needed was a run-in with the law, Mexican or U.S. How could he have been such an idiot?

In a pocket of his new leather vest, Nena found a fat joint and flushed it down the toilet. She turned the pocket inside out, daubed it clean with a cotton ball dipped in Cal's aftershave, and flushed it, too.

Just as she was falling asleep, a loud knock came at the door. "*¿Quién?*" she called out.

"*¡Judiciales!* Federal police. Open up!"

Nena sat up with a start. When the voice at the door repeated the command even more loudly and emphatically, she knew she wasn't dreaming. Trembling, she called out, "*¡Ahí voy!* I'll be right there!" She switched on a light, reached into the closet for a robe, and put it on over her nightgown. Cal stirred in his sleep and muttered something unintelligible.

She peered through the peephole and saw two uniformed Mexican judiciales, one holding the leash of a large German Shepherd. Her heart pounding loudly, she unlatched the lock and opened the door to the two beefy policemen. She politely asked them what they wanted.

The cop holding the dog couldn't pry his eyes off Nena's chest, where the robe had fallen open. She gripped the neck closed and cinched the sash tighter around her waist. In a gruff voice, the other cop, who seemed to be in charge, asked to see her documents and those of her *compañero,* pronouncing the word sarcastically as he nodded toward the sleeping Cal. Nena fetched their passports from the dresser. The cop with the dog stepped in, gave a command in a low voice, and unhooked the dog's leash. It eagerly began sniffing around the room.

Cal sat up in bed with a jolt. "Jesus! What the fuck's going on?" he said, clutching the covers to his chest as, terror-stricken, he watched the huge dog's muzzle graze the bedspread.

"Let me handle this, Cal. Please don't say anything," she implored. "Please."

She handed their passports to the policeman in charge and began to speak to him in her best and most polite Spanish. "I think you'll find that our documents are all in order, sir. This is most unusual. I've never heard of police coming to tourists' rooms in the middle of the night."

The policeman grunted as he leafed through her passport. "In the U.S., police frequently come to Mexican citizens' homes in the middle of the night, asking to see their papers," he said. "Or they visit them where they are working."

"With all due respect, Officer, I think this is a little different. We're tourists—not immigrants. If you have any questions about who we are, I suggest you call my uncle in Dolores Hidalgo, Francisco Herrera, the chief of police."

Startled, the policeman looked up. "Don Paco? The winner of the Olympic medal? You're his niece?"

"Yes," Nena said. "He's my mother's brother, and we're on our way tomorrow to visit him. Here—we can call him right now on this telephone."

The policeman with the dog approached his colleague. *"Nada,"* he said quietly.

The officer in charge nervously returned the passports and tipped his hat to her. "Please forgive us, señora," he said earnestly, his eyes wide with alarm. "We're so sorry to have disturbed you. There has been a terrible misunderstanding, a case of mistaken identity. We were looking for a couple wanted in the U.S. for drug smuggling. Our informants obviously gave us erroneous information."

She nodded, her arms crossed tightly over her chest as she tried to contain her trembling.

The policeman was genuinely chagrined. *"¡Discúlpenos, por favor, señora!"* he repeated. "In Mexico, we're trying very hard to root out the drug menace, with the help of your American DEA. Unfortunately, errors can occur. Please do not let this regrettable incident ruin your vacation in our country. You have our deepest apologies. Your uncle is well known to us, he's highly respected in this region and throughout Mexico, and we are very, very sorry to have bothered one of his family members."

Nena accepted the policemen's apologies, and they left quickly with the dog in tow.

She closed and locked the door behind them, and collapsed into an armchair, letting out a long exhalation of relief.

"What the fuck was that all about?" Cal muttered.

She glowered at him, digging her fingernails into the arms of the chair. "Your incredible stupidity," she said between clenched teeth.

35

In bed, Nena tossed and turned for what seemed like hours beside Cal, who snored and lay motionless as a felled oak. At dawn, she got up and dressed in her jogging gear. A run would help dispel the night's tensions.

The hotel lobby was empty, except for a workman pushing an old-fashioned carpet sweeper through the foyer. Outside, a cool, clean breeze greeted her. She set off, her pace light and easy as she trotted through the half-lit shadows of the Jardín's trees, past shuttered restaurants and vacant park benches. In front of the exuberantly decorated old Teatro Juárez opera house, she veered onto the main street and followed it in the direction of the Plaza de la Paz. She hadn't gone a block when, up ahead, facing her way, she saw a familiar-looking black Bronco with Texas plates straddling the empty sidewalk. The driver was leaning out his window, conversing with a woman in red sweats, who had a foot propped up on the truck's running board. As Nena approached, the driver saw her and started up his engine. The woman in red turned to stare and tossed her cigarette into the street.

"Buenos días, María," Nena called cheerfully as she jogged past. The driver rolled up his tinted window quickly, but not before she caught a glimpse of his scarred cheek. She felt a surge of triumph at catching María in the act of conferring with Scarface. Ever since Nelson took their picture in Tepotzotlán, she felt the couple, the norteños, and the DEA guys had to be connected. Following her to Mexico with Cal. Trying to set them up on drug charges. There was no doubt in her mind that this crew was responsible for the midnight raid with the judiciales, and the source of the "erroneous information" to which the policeman referred. Well, it didn't work. None of it did. The minute she got home she was going to the authorities. Her will was steeled.

Anger and determination surged through Nena. She picked up her pace, her feet pouncing on the pavement, her lungs seizing the early morning air as she lengthened her stride. She ran fast through Guanajuato's unpopulated streets, racing right and left and right again into little side streets, losing track of her direction until she found herself in the alley behind the Posada. She slowed to a walk and entered the hotel, her heart thumping loudly and blood pulsing through her legs as her breath came in gasps.

Cal was still sound asleep when she let herself in. She stripped off her sweaty clothes and went into the bathroom for a shower. A quarter-hour later, she came out, enveloped in a cloud of steam and wrapped in a large white towel, fluffing her hair dry with a smaller one.

Cal rolled over and looked at Nena with bleary, gummy eyes. "Oh my God," he said, as he draped his forearm over his brow. "What hit me?"

Nena sat down in an armchair opposite Cal to brush her hair. "It might have been the dope, Doctor Banner. La mota?"

Cal moaned loudly. "No," he said. "I think it was the tequila. They were showing me the salt, lime, and shots routine. God, my head feels like it's going to burst! I'm too old for this."

"Do you remember the cops, Cal?"

He groaned.

"Do you have any idea why they might have come to our room?"

"Don't bitch at me. I said I feel like shit. Cut me some slack!"

"It was scary, Cal. I was terrified. Can you imagine what kind of problems your marijuana possession could have caused us? Could have caused *me*? What kind of repercussions there might have been for us—for *me*—back in the U.S.? Like losing my job at the university?" Nena was quaking with anger. "Like you losing your job? Do you think you'd get tenure anywhere with a drug charge on your resumé, Doctor Banner?"

Without removing his arm from his forehead or even glancing her way, Cal said, "I apologize, Nena, for whatever I might have done that caused those police to come to our room. Is that what you want me to say—I'm sorry? There, I said it. Are you happy now?"

She didn't reply. She sat quietly for several minutes, soothing herself as she methodically brushed the tangles out of her hair. Cal probably didn't even remember the joint. Somebody might have put it into his vest pocket without his knowledge.

He moaned again. "Oh, sweet Jesus, I feel dreadful."

She sighed through pursed lips. "I'm going downstairs to have breakfast, Cal. I'm starving. Are you coming?"

"Breakfast—I can't even begin to think about food. The room is still spinning around. Ohhhhhh, I think I'm going to be sick!" Throwing off the bedclothes, Cal made a dash for the bathroom.

Nena grimaced as she heard him retching and vomiting. She had no sympathy for him. He was making a habit of hangovers. She dressed quickly. "I'll be in the dining room," she called out as she closed the door behind her.

Cal never appeared at breakfast. After finishing a hearty meal of papaya juice, *chilaquiles,* and coffee, Nena returned to the room.

He was still in bed, and turned over to face her. "Don't say anything," he said, shielding his eyes with one arm, while waving the other in her general direction. "I don't need any more of your annoying, supercilious diatribes this morning."

"I was going to ask you if I could get you anything—aspirin, coffee, juice. Maybe I shouldn't disappoint you by being nice. In fact, maybe I should tell you what a moron you are." Nena plopped down in the overstuffed armchair by the window.

Cal waggled a finger at her. "Don't start, goddammit."

She took a deep breath and looked out over Guanajuato's rooftops to the brilliant blue sky above. "Can I get you anything, Cal? Seriously."

"Just leave me alone," he mumbled.

"Ooooooh-kay. The only thing is, we were going to leave for Dolores Hidalgo this afternoon. Will you be back in the land of the living by then? Check-out is probably around one."

"I'll be fine. Now, pull those damn drapes shut, and let me sleep."

36

Not wanting to waste what was left of the beautiful morning, Nena strolled through the city's bustling streets and followed signs to the Diego Rivera Museum. The narrow row house, where he and his twin brother were born in 1886, now honored the painter and displayed examples of his work. Nena toured all three floors, lingering over his earliest sketches, which clearly showed his artistic promise. In the gift shop on the first floor, she picked out postcards of her favorite flower vendor paintings.

Nelson suddenly appeared at her elbow. "How nice to see you this morning," he said obsequiously. "Can I interest you in a coffee?"

Nena hesitated. In the worst way she wanted to scream, "Fuck off, cretin! Your dope-planting scheme didn't work. Whoever you are, I've had enough of your bullshit. And you should damn well leave me alone!" But she didn't want to cause a scene.

"Thank you. No. I really need time to myself this morning."

"Oh, come on," Nelson whined. "A nice cup of coffee? Maybe we go find María?"

"No, thank you," she said firmly. "Now if you don't mind . . ." She brushed past him and approached the counter with her postcards.

"No problem," Nelson said cheerfully. "Maybe we see you later." With a large, toothy grin, he walked past her and out the door.

"I certainly hope not," she muttered, loud enough for him to hear as well as the other people in the shop. She knew she was being rude, but she had no desire to spend a single second more in his company, or María's.

Nena strolled down Positos Street and found a table in a friendly, boisterous café, where she sipped lemonade and wrote postcards. At noon, when she returned to the hotel, Cal was dressing. "How are you feeling?" she asked.

"Like death on toast," Cal groused.

"Maybe some soup would do you good. *Menudo pa' tu cruda.* A bowl of menudo would fix you right up."

Cal put on his dark glasses. "What's menudo?"

"Tripe soup."

Cal gagged.

*   *   *   *   *

Though they were early for lunch—Mexican lunch hour being one-thirty or later—Nena talked the waiter at the Restaurant Valadez into bringing Cal a bowl of chicken soup.

"Are you up for the ride to Dolores?" she asked, watching him slowly spoon soup into his mouth with a trembling hand.

"Can't we stay here another day?"

"It's just that my family's expecting us late this afternoon."

Cal moaned. "Frankly, Nena, the last thing I feel like doing today is visiting your Mexican relatives. I'd rather spend the day lolling about the hotel. Moreover, I haven't seen anything of the town."

"That's not my fault."

"Don't piss me off!" Cal said angrily.

"If we stay here another day, we'll be rushed. Our flight leaves from Mexico City in three days. Didn't you realize that one of my main reasons for this trip was to see my family? Not to mention the fact that it was my uncle's name that saved us from big hassles last night."

Cal slurped his soup. "It was clearly a case of mistaken identity. Isn't that what you told me the cops said?"

Nena rested her chin on her folded hands and watched Cal eat. "They were looking for a person with marijuana on him. Could that be anyone you know?"

He looked up. "Let's not discuss this, Nena. That was an absolutely terrifying experience, and it would never have happened in a civilized country."

Nena sighed. It was pointless to try to talk to him about the events of the night before. He probably couldn't remember much anyway. She decided to change the subject. "If you like, we can still sightsee a bit before we head for Dolores. It's only an hour from here. We have all afternoon."

Cal hailed a waiter and ordered a beer. Nena frowned, but held her tongue.

He looked at her over the tops of his sunglasses. "I feel shitty. . . . You could at least be sympathetic. Hair of the dog that bit me—it'll make me feel better." He perked up after he drank the first beer and ordered another.

"I'm going back to the hotel," Nena said. "I guess we're not going to make the one o'clock check-out. I'll see if they'll give us another couple of hours. Usually they will."

"Capital idea, m'dear. See you later."

37

It was well after three before they checked out. Cal was still hung-over and grumpy even after several beers, lunch, and a nap. He sat on the passenger side, slumped against the car door, his eyes shut, his arms crossed over his chest in a death pose. Nena maneuvered the VW through the city's clogged, chaotic streets, humming a little tune to herself, trying to dislodge her own malaise, a hollow-headed feeling caused by last night's terrifying encounter with the police and her deep disappointment at Cal's ongoing idiocy.

Looking back over her shoulder, she was not surprised to discover the black Bronco a half block behind her. She gritted her teeth and sped up. The Bronco gained quickly on her, until it was only a few feet from her rear bumper. In the mirror, she could clearly see the driver, the blond man with glasses. The bearded man with the scar was in the passenger seat. Both of them looked angry and tense.

"Goddamn it!" Nena slapped the steering wheel.

Cal opened his eyes. "Now what?"

"If I thought you'd believe me, I'd tell you we're being followed," she said.

Alarmed, Cal turned around just as Nena gunned the engine, and the VW lurched forward. Traveling fast, she wove in and out of traffic, making a screeching series of lefts and rights.

Tossed from side to side, Cal began to protest. " Have you lost your mind? Followed? Followed by whom? Slow down, for Chrissakes! You're making me seasick. Is this the way to Dolores . . . wherever the hell we're going?"

Nena didn't reply. The Bronco was sticking with her, and the men in the front seat now seemed to be enjoying themselves, grinning triumphantly like predators closing in on their prey. The VW was nimble and better able to negotiate Guanajuato's jumbled streets than their huge, boxy, swaying vehicle, but Nena doubted she'd be able to lose them. Then she had an idea. With the Bronco close on her tail, she drove up a steep hillside where the streets became increasingly narrower. Finally, she spied what she'd been looking for. She rounded a corner almost on two wheels, and shot into an unpaved alleyway that soon tapered until the space between the tottering old buildings was barely wide enough for the VW.

"What the fuck are you doing?" Cal shrieked as the car bounded down the funnel-shaped lane.

She glanced quickly in her rear-view mirror and grinned. The Bronco followed her into the alley. She accelerated.

Cal swiveled in his seat and peered out the rear window. "Who are those men behind us? What's going on?"

Suddenly, there was a loud crunching, scraping sound behind them, and a horn blared angrily.

"Oh, Christ, Nena. Those men just got wedged between two buildings! And are they pissed! I don't think they can even open their doors. They're shaking their fists at us. What the hell is this all about?"

Nena chuckled and kept driving. "Chalk up one for our side!" she said triumphantly. "Yahoo!"

"You're fucking nuts," Cal said.

Up and down the street, heads popped out of windows at the commotion. People tumbled out of shops and houses, shouting and waving their arms excitedly. Converging on the stuck vehicle, they roared with delight, laughing and pointing at the enraged, red-faced gringos trapped in the front seat. Neighborhood dogs joined in, barking and howling, adding to the clamor of crowing roosters, mocking children, and the vroom, vroom of a powerful engine being gunned fruitlessly.

"I demand that you tell me what's going on!" Cal barked. His face was red, his fists clenched in anger.

She ignored him. Her jaw set in determination and her hands firmly guiding the car, she drove on as fast as possible, the VW tilting and bouncing on squealing springs as it splashed from one muddy pothole to another. Over the whine of her engine, she could still hear the Bronco's angry, frustrated roar. At the end of the block, she zipped out of the alley, turned left onto a paved road and headed back downhill to one of the main streets that would lead her out of Guanajuato.

Cal was incensed. "You did that on purpose. You fully intended to get those fellows stuck back there. Who are they? What the fuck have you done?" His face was purple with rage.

Nena said nothing.

"Stop this car!" Cal yelled. "Stop right now!"

She sped on for another block and stopped beside a small park. Her engine idling, she sat motionless, her arms draped over the wheel.

"You're out of your fucking mind," Cal ranted. "Whoever those men are, they're bound to be mad as hornets after what you did to them. Their car is probably badly scraped. Their paint job is wrecked. They can't even get out of their car. They'll need a tow truck to get out of there. What the hell is the matter with you? Get out. I'm driving, goddammit!"

"No, you're not," Nena said placidly.

"Get out!" Cal shouted.

Passersby turned to gape open-mouthed at the foreign couple fighting inside the Volkswagen. Children peered into the car's windows and giggled, covering their mouths with their hands.

"I have a better idea," Nena said. "You get out. And take your luggage, too, Doctor Banner. Maybe I'll see you back in Mexico City—maybe not."

Cal stared at her wide-eyed, his jaw dropping in astonishment.

Nena rounded on him. Her eyes were fierce and unsmiling. "You heard me. Get out," she hissed between clenched teeth. "I rented this car. It's mine. Out!"

"How am I supposed to get back to Mexico City?" Cal wailed.

"You can catch the bus, Doctor Banner. With the proletariat."

"The *bus?*"

She pulled a lever that popped the hood. "Get your suitcase, Cal. Now."

He began to open his door. "I do believe you're serious." He was incredulous.

"I am absolutely serious. Take your luggage and go. This is the end of the trail, cowboy."

Cal clambered out of the Volkswagen, jerked his bag out of the trunk, and angrily slammed the hood down. He walked around to the driver's side, leaned over, and started to say something to Nena. With a squeal of rubber, the VW leaped forward, leaving him speechless, enveloped in a cloud of exhaust and dust.

38

Nena was exhilarated. Invigorated. Liberated. Giddy even. She would never, ever forget the look on Cal Banner's face when she told him to get out of her car. It was priceless! Shock, outrage, anger, and anxiety all mixed in one delicious, delectable vision she'd treasure forever. It was almost as precious to her as the scene in her rear view mirror that showed the fury on the DEA guys' faces as they realized their mighty macho machine was stuck fast between two buildings.

Whistling a little mariachi tune, Nena wound her way through Guanajuato's streets, searching for signs to Dolores Hidalgo.

The truth was now painfully obvious. She should have dumped Banner much, much sooner. To think she had once found the man fascinating, charming and—ugh!—sexy. How could she have been so blind for so long? Cal Banner was a jackass. A pompous, self-absorbed asshole. She giggled as she recalled his astonishment when she suggested he take the bus back to Mexico City. Well, it would do him good to have to find his own way back to "civilization."

Nena followed a main street uphill. She shifted gears and the pitch of the Volkswagen's engine switched to a higher whine as the little car valiantly ascended the sharp incline. She believed this was the right road to Dolores Hidalgo, but she wasn't certain. On top of the escarpment, the street began to meander through a barrio of half-finished cement-block houses, jumbled shacks, and roadside stands. When the street petered out into a dirt road, she knew she must have made a wrong turn. She searched for someone who could give her directions, but except for a few bony dogs and children playing in puddles by the roadside, the streets were deserted. She wasn't really worried. The road was heading north—she could tell by the splash of sunset colors along the horizon to her left. Sooner or later she'd find her way to the main highway. Fortunately, she had filled up the VW's tank while Cal slept back in the hotel.

The well-traveled dirt track soon veered onto a narrow asphalt road. Nena was relieved. She drove on, looking in vain for signs or a person who might send her in the right direction. The roadway was as devoid of people as the countryside though which it now wandered. Whole regions of Mexico had been deserted by campesinos migrating to cities or to the U.S. The state of Guanajuato, in particular, had lost much of its rural population.

Dusk soon descended, and Nena was getting nervous. Ahead, in the last of the daylight, she saw two straw-hatted figures standing beside their bicycles at the edge of the road. She slowed to a stop. Reaching around behind her, she grasped the shopping bag containing her uncle's gun and set it on the passenger seat beside her. Campesinos were usually polite and trustworthy, but she was far from any settlement, a foreign woman lost and alone. It wouldn't hurt to be cautious. The two men turned at her approach.

Leaving the engine running, she rolled down her window, greeted them politely, and asked for directions to the road to Dolores Hidalgo, *Carretera 110*.

"*¿Usted está perdida?*" the older man asked with a bemused smile. He seemed to think it was funny that she was lost. The other man, young enough to be his son, stared at Nena obliquely, shyly.

"*Solo un poquito perdida,*" she said with a smile. "I'm only a little lost."

Both of the men pointed north and east. "*Por allí,*" they said in unison.

"The carretera's not far from here," the younger one added. "Continue on straight ahead. This road eventually meets up with it."

"*Gracias, señores, muy amables,*" she said.

Campesinos seldom owned vehicles and were often vague about distances. Still, unless they were mistaken, she'd soon be on the right road. She breathed a sigh of relief, and the hollow feeling in her stomach subsided.

With a wave, she drove off, heading north, traversing a vacant, rolling countryside that in the dusky light was studded with the shadowy forms of mesquite, cacti, and rocky outcroppings.

*   *   *   *   *

A few miles down the road, she noticed a pair of headlights growing larger in her rear view mirror. A vehicle was rapidly gaining on her. Cresting a hill, she rounded a curve and slowed as she came into a small, deserted village. Her brakes squealed as she downshifted and bounced over a *tope,* a speed bump laid across the road beneath a solitary street lamp. Several blocks further on, at the far edge of the village, as she neared a second tope, she happened to check her rear view mirror, and a stab of fear shot through her. Back at the entrance to the village, the black Bronco was hiccupping over the first speed bump.

How on earth had they found her? She didn't even know where she was, other than in the State of Guanajuato. There hadn't been anyone behind her for miles. She was certain of that. Then it struck her that if these men were intent on following her, as they certainly were, maybe they'd put an electronic tracking device on her car.

Her heart raced as she put the VW through its gears and sped on into the growing darkness, hoping she wasn't far from the heavily-traveled main highway or a larger town where she could seek refuge. She wasn't hopeful of being able to outrun the Bronco in her putt-putt rental car.

Nena tightened her grip on the steering wheel and urged the car to go faster. She was furious with herself for being so naïve. The guys in the Bronco who had tailed her in Mexico were cops— dirty cops. Pepe was right to warn her, and now she wished she'd listened to him. These men were murderers. They deliberately caused Chuck LaCour's plane crash. They knew Nena overheard them plotting and was a witness to their conspiracy. They knew she planned to turn them in when she got back to Albuquerque. Their attempt to set her up for a drug bust had failed. And now they were after her to . . . what? Have a friendly chat with her out in the Mexican desert?

The VW's engine protested as Nena pressed her foot to the floor and raced onward through a desert that in all directions was blue-black and deathly still. Her headlights illuminated cactus spikes that poked up out of the hardscrabble earth like quills on a porcupine's back. Stars glittered like thousands of knife-points scattered over an inky sky that stretched beyond the silhouettes of jagged mountains. The air coming in her open window was ice-edged. There were no lights anywhere except the headlights in her rear-view mirror growing larger and brighter. Without warning, a coyote dashed in front of her. She swerved to the right, missing him by what must have been inches, her tires skimming the pavement's edge. In a blur of silver, the coyote disappeared into the chaparral. Nena's heart beat wildly, racing along with her straining engine. She forced herself to take deep breaths in a useless effort to control her terror.

The old highway crested a rise, then tipped downward. Along the western horizon, the last faint glow of twilight showed her the road ahead narrowing as it approached a bridge spanning a deep, dark gash in the earth. The Bronco was gaining on her. She begged the VW to go faster and faster, but her pursuers continued to come up hard on her tail. Suddenly, a jolt from behind slammed Nena forward into the wheel, then back into the seat. They'd tapped the rear of her car. She fought to stay on the road and again floored the VW. The Bronco dropped back. Then it came at her again, now striking with more force. The VW bucked hard. Nena's head felt like it was going to snap loose from her neck. Using all the strength in her arms, she took the only defensive measure she could think of, swerving her car from left to right, in an attempt to evade their charges. Again they backed off. Just as she reached the point where the road narrowed to a single lane at the bridge's edge, they came up hard and fast alongside her on the left. Without a moment's hesitation, Nena thrust her right hand into the shopping bag on the passenger seat, jerked out the .38, and blindly fired the gun repeatedly across her body at the Bronco.

The gun's reports and the explosion of glass were deafening, followed by a loud crash that ricocheted through Nena's ringing ears, then another and another. The Bronco plunged over the canyon rim, its headlights gyrating wildly as it tumbled through the air, plummeting down into the chasm, careening off cliffs in a cascade of crumpled metal, down, down into the deep darkness below the bridge.

Convulsed with tremors, her ears throbbing with pain from the gun's deafening discharge, Nena took her foot off the accelerator and the VW coasted to a halt. To her surprise, she was now on the far end of the bridge. Barely able to control her shaking, she put the car into neutral and set the hand brake. With unwilling fingers, she undid her seatbelt, fumbled for the door handle, and let herself out. Her legs were like gelatin, and she nearly fell to her knees when her feet hit the pavement.

She stumbled back onto the bridge and peered over the railing into the chasm. Even in the darkness she could see clouds of smoke billowing up from the canyon floor hundreds of feet below. Like an alien force, a horrible animal sound welled up from deep inside her and fought its way out into the black night. Nena keened, her own eerie wail raising the hairs on her arms and the back of her neck. Fear pulsed through every part of her like shots of iced blood.

Then all of a sudden, she sensed that she was not alone. An invisible presence wrapped itself around her, and a bony hand firmly gripped her forearm the way Libertad often had when Nena was about to run into a cactus or step on a snake. Robot-like and staggering, she let herself be guided back over the bridge into the VW, her boneless legs barely able to support her.

Although her fingers were unresponsive sticks of lead, and the throbbing in her chest and ears pounded at her in waves, Nena managed to release the brake and put the car in gear. Slowly and mechanically, she drove away from the scene.

39

She had no idea how she found her way to her aunt and uncle's house in Dolores Hidalgo. Later, she recalled sitting like an automaton behind the wheel, while the car drove itself through heavy truck traffic on a busy highway. There were startlingly bright city lights and slower traffic, then narrower streets that seemed familiar, a house with all its lights ablaze, and at last, the warm arms of her aunt and uncle enveloping her as she tumbled out of the car.

Huddled in a blanket in her aunt's arms on the sofa in their living room, Nena spoke in a small, tremulous voice. "First, you have to promise me you will never tell my mother," she said.

They reluctantly agreed.

Nena took a deep breath. "A few weeks ago, I had a hideous nightmare. It was about that bridge in the desert. You know the one. Over the gorge south of here. I knew something awful would happen there. And now it has!" she sobbed.

Tia Lourdes helped her sip a cup of *manzanilla* tea. "Tell us what happened," she said gently.

Nena babbled out her story, beginning with the customs office conversation. When she came to the part about getting lost on her way to Dolores Hidalgo and the Bronco's unforeseen appearance, she began to quiver and cry.

"You don't have to talk now, hija," her aunt said, rocking Nena in her arms like a baby, smoothing her hair back from her forehead.

"No," Nena said, getting a grip on herself. "I have to tell you everything. They must have put an electronic tracer on my VW, because all of a sudden, out in the middle of nowhere, there they were, right on my tail. There was no way I could outrun them. It was terrifying.

"First they toyed with me, like a cat with a mouse. They tapped my car with their bumper, not hard enough to knock me off the road, but enough to rattle me badly. Then they hit me harder. We approached the bridge and I guess they decided to go for broke and shove me into the canyon. They swerved alongside just as we reached the bridge, and that's when I shot at them!" Nena began to sob and wail. "What if they're still alive trapped down in that canyon?"

As his wife held Nena closer, kissing her forehead, Paco spoke. "No way, m'hija. It's nearly a hundred meters down to the bottom of that canyon. Every year, people drive off that bridge, and nobody ever survives the drop."

"Then I killed them. I murdered two men!" She repeated again and again. "How can I ever live with myself?"

Her uncle reached for her hands and held them tightly in his. "Listen to me. It was them or you, Coyota. You have nothing to feel sorry for. Your survival instincts simply took over, you fought hard for your own life, and you won. It was God's will. They were murderers. They were out to kill you, like they killed your student, and they met a just fate."

"What's going to happen to me, Tío Paco? Will I be indicted for murder?"

"Nothing's going to happen to you, Nena. You were obviously completely justified in doing what you did. I know you. I know you'd never intentionally harm anyone."

"Yes, but what's a court going to think? Am I going to spend the rest of my life in a Mexican prison?"

Paco took a deep breath and exchanged looks with his wife. "I frankly don't see any reason to report the incident and put you through what could be very ugly formalities, m'hija. It's doubtful there were any witnesses to the accident, and it could be days before anyone notices the new damage to the bridge or spies the Bronco down in the canyon. Sooner or later, though, somebody's going to report those men missing. From what you say, they were traveling with others.

"The two DEA agents were alone in the Bronco, though. I'm sure of that," Nena said.

"I think you should leave Mexico immediately. That's the safest thing. I'll drive you up to the border myself. Luis can meet us in El Paso to take you home to Corrales."

"Ay, Tío, you're sure those men couldn't be alive down in that barranca?"

"No, there's no way they're still alive, believe me. Maybe now we'll get a decent bridge. The state doesn't care about poor *guanajuatenses* tumbling into that ravine in our beat-to-shit trocas. But maybe the death of a couple of gringos—¡chotas!—will convince the governor we need a two-lane bridge there."

"What about the VW?"

"I'll have your cousin, Chuy, look for the transponder right now. Cops usually put them on the inside of a bumper. *Los bumper beepers,* we call them. Once he has it, he can transfer it to a bus or truck going out of town to fool anyone who might be monitoring your car's whereabouts. First thing in the morning, he'll drive the VW to Mexico City, where he can get it fixed. Once it's repaired, he'll take it back to Budget for you. They'll never know the difference. Chuy's going to university in the D.F. in the fall, and he welcomes any opportunity to go to the capital. My own son wants to abandon his beautiful native state and become a chilango. What do you think of that?"

Nena smiled.

"Ah, a smile," her aunt said, squeezing her. "You're going to be fine, *linda*. Soon you'll be back home, and all of this will be like a bad dream."

Tears spilled down Nena's cheeks. "I wish it were just a nightmare, Tía Lourdes."

"I think we should leave as soon as possible for the border," Paco said. "Lourdes, can you make us a thermos of coffee and some *tortas?* I'll go gas up the car, and maybe I can find a *farmacia* open. A little Valium would be good for you, Nena. You've had a terrible shock. It will help you sleep in the car."

"I don't feel right about you driving all the way to the border, Tío Paco. Isn't it about twenty hours each way?"

Paco shrugged. *"Menos.* A lot less."

"Why not put me on a bus? It's awfully far to Juárez, and I'm sure you have other things to do. I don't want you to get into trouble because of me."

Paco bristled. "You're my niece, and I'm not going to feel right until I know you're safely across the border and on your way home with Luis. Speaking of your brother, I should call him right now."

"What day is it?" Nena asked.

"It's Friday, linda," Lourdes said.

"He'll be at Rosa's dad's house, playing poker with the guys. I have the phone number in my address book, in my purse."

*   *   *   *   *

It was after midnight when Nena's cousin, Chuy, loaded her luggage and his father's gym bag into the trunk of the family's Ford sedan. One of Paco's deputies accompanied them on their trip north, to help with the driving.

"I've got important business to tend to in El Paso," Paco told the deputy. "And my American niece is sick and needs to get home fast."

Nena looked ill. She was shaky, her face puffy and pale, her eyes red-rimmed. Before she got into the car, she handed Chuy her Mexican pesos and a couple hundred dollars, the last of her cash. He tried to refuse the money, but she insisted. "I don't know if this will be enough to pay for the damage to the VW."

"It's way more than enough, Nena. There are dozens of auto graveyards around Mexico City, and zillions of VW parts to choose from. No sweat."

Tears filled Nena's eyes as she hugged her cousin and her aunt good-bye. "I was so excited about spending time with you. And now this!"

"Don't worry, prima," Chuy said. "There'll be another time."

Nena wasn't so sure she would ever come back to Guanajuato—or even to Mexico. But she nodded, got into the car, and rolled down her window. "You're all being so generous. I can't tell you how much you mean to me."

"Somos familia," Tía Lourdes said. "That's what family is for."

40

Nena slept for hours as they drove north to Ciudad Juárez. She woke briefly when Tío Paco or the deputy slowed to pay tolls, or when they stopped for gas, then fell back into a troubled, half-drugged sleep. The terrifying vision of the Bronco plummeting into the canyon continually invaded her mind, making her weep. Her ears still rang with the deafening sound of gunfire and the crash of metal careening off rock, and her stomach was queasy with fright–the horror of what lay behind her, and the fear of what might lie ahead.

By mid-morning, they were outside of Torreón. When they stopped for gas, Nena went into the restaurant to use the bathroom. She looked in the mirror and recoiled. She barely recognized herself. She was a mess. Her hair was tangled like a tumbleweed, her skin was blotchy, and her eyes were nearly swollen shut. She wet paper towels with cold water and pressed them to her eyes in an attempt to get the swelling to go down. She washed her face, combed out her hair, and put on a dab of lipstick.

As she came out of the restaurant, Paco said, "Ah, you must be feeling better, niña. Maybe you should eat. How about a torta?"

At the mention of food, she found she was ravenously hungry. She accepted one of her aunt's chicken sandwiches and climbed back into the rear seat of the car. After eating and downing a can of lukewarm Pepsi, she curled up and tried to go back to sleep.

From time to time, whether she was dozing or simply taking

in the bleak landscape that flowed past her window, Nena could feel the deputy's eyes on her in the rear view mirror. Tío Paco had surely not told him what happened. No doubt he was wondering about the hastily planned trip north with the jefe's niece who looked like hell.

At Villa Ahumada, Paco parked in front of a row of open-air food stands strung out along the road. Nena stayed in the back seat while her uncle and the deputy stood beside one of the stands, filling up on *chicharrón* tacos. While her uncle went off in search of a bathroom, Nena got out of the car and spoke to the deputy. "I appreciate you making this trip with us," she said, combing her hair back from her face with her fingers.

The deputy, a short, pudgy, nervous young man, brightened. "Oh, it's no trouble, señorita. Your uncle's a fine man. I'm happy to be of service to him and to you."

"I had a terrible experience with my boyfriend in Guanajuato," Nena said, making up a plausible story on the spot. "He's very jealous, very violent. I had to leave quickly."

The deputy was dismayed. "I'm sorry for you. You'll feel better as soon as you're home in the States with your family."

Paco returned. Nena took his arm. "I was explaining to your deputy that I had a terrible experience with my boyfriend back in Guanajuato, Tío Paco. That's why I'm such a wreck."

Paco smiled. "You'll be over it soon, Nena. I keep telling my niece she needs a new boyfriend, Sánchez."

"At last I agree with you, Tío," Nena said.

The deputy excused himself.

Taking advantage of his absence, Paco outlined for Nena his plan to help her cross the border safely. "We'll drop you off in the old market in downtown Juárez, where you should buy things a day-tripping tourist might buy—paper flowers, a tote bag, souvenir trinkets. Then you take a taxi through the checkpoint and go to the Del Norte Hotel in El Paso, where Luis will be waiting for you. Meanwhile, Sánchez and I will drive my car over the bridge with your luggage and meet you at the hotel.

"Why don't we just drive through the checkpoint together?"

"With Guanajuato plates, we're sure to get stopped and questioned by U.S. Customs, m'hija. It's unlikely they're watching for you, but it's a possibility. If you cross by yourself as a turista in a taxi during rush hour, with no luggage and a shopping bag full of artesanías, they won't give you a second glance. They probably won't even ask you your name."

"How are you going to explain carrying a suitcase full of women's clothes if customs opens my luggage?" Nena grinned.

Paco cogitated for a second. "I'll say it's my daughter's, and she's visiting relatives in El Paso. We'll make one more stop to gas up before we get to Juárez. That'll be your opportunity to get rid of anything that shows you were in the Mexican interior—hotel receipts, charge slips, the airline baggage tag on your suitcase. ¿De acuerdo?"

Nena nodded her agreement. Her uncle seemed overly cautious, but she was happy to go along with his plan.

"Oh, and here's fifty dollars. I saw you give all your money to Chuy," Paco said. "You'll need this for the souvenirs."

Soon, a red sun was sliding behind the horizon, tingeing the big sand dunes of the Jornada del Muerto south of Juárez the color of watery blood. Nena grew tense thinking about crossing the border. "What's there to be afraid of?" She chastised herself. But customs could be an enemy, and in order to get home safely, she had to get past them.

Sánchez drove, his arms casually looped over the steering wheel. Paco turned in the passenger seat, reached for Nena's hand and held it firmly in his. He spoke in English. "No worry, Nena. Everything is fine. Your brother is waiting for you in El Paso. We have a big drink together at the Del Norte, and soon you be home in your own house."

Nena nodded. The throbbing in her ears made everything she heard fade in and out like a bad radio signal.

By the time they reached the old market in Juárez, many of the vendors were rolling iron shutters down over the entrances to their stands, closing up for the night.

"*Apúrate,* Nena. You'd better hurry. I'll find you a reliable taxi while you buy the turista things," Paco said.

Nena hastily bought a jute market bag and filled it with a large bundle of brightly colored paper flowers, adding to it a couple of jars of cajeta, the gooey goat's milk caramel her mother loved. For her office mates at the university, a big jar of Nescafé instant espresso, a more potent, tastier brew than the American version. She quickly grabbed two goofy Cantinflas marionettes, several Tarahumara Indian baskets, and a dozen tiny pine bark-and-cloth dolls off a vendor's shelves, and paid for them. On her way out, she hesitated at a fruit stand, contemplating mangoes and pineapples. They smelled ripe and delicious. But fruit would provoke questions at customs. She left the market.

When Nena returned to Tío Paco's car, a Juárez taxi was waiting for her. Her uncle gave her a big abrazo, opened the taxi door, and helped her into the back seat with her bulging shopping bag.

"We'll see you in a while," he said to Nena, closing the door. "The taxi's paid for, and he'll take you right to the Del Norte."

"Ay, Tío," Nena frowned. "You do too much for me."

He grinned and saluted as the taxi drove off in the direction of the Stanton Street Bridge, the nearest border crossing.

*   *   *   *   *

At the bridge that spanned the garbage-strewn, nearly dry Río Grande, early evening traffic was backed up for several blocks in wobbly stop-and-go lines. Crimson brake lights on the hundreds of cars and trucks waiting to cross the border winked on and off in the dusk like Christmas lights as the vehicles stuttered forward toward waiting border officials. Nena's taxi slowly approached the customs post. For a moment she wished she had taken another Valium to calm her nerves, but she knew it was best to appear alert, rather than drugged out. With her face and eyes still puffy, she probably looked bad enough as it was. She took her cosmetic bag out of her purse, refreshed her lipstick, and ran a brush through her mussed hair.

Ahead, traffic separated into neater lanes to file through the border station. Nena's driver chose a lane in the middle of the stream and inched forward. As they drew closer to the American side of the bridge, she could see a U.S. Customs official standing outside his booth, leaning into the open window of each car or truck as it drew alongside. Her stomach tightened and her heart began to beat faster.

When it was her taxi's turn, the official, a paunchy, gray-haired man in steel-rimmed glasses, peered into the back seat. "Where you from, ma'am?" he asked with a Texas drawl as his eyes inspected every inch of the interior.

"Albuquerque," Nena said brightly, her nerves firmly under control.

"Is that where you were born?"

"Yes, sir. St. Joseph's Hospital."

"And what did you purchase in Mexico, ma'am?"

"Just a few gifts, sir. A couple of marionettes, a dozen little dolls, baskets—oh, and the paper flowers. I really love paper flowers."

"Did you purchase any alcohol or fruit in Mexico?"

"No, sir."

"What is the total value of your purchases?"

"Uh, maybe about forty dollars, sir. Well no, maybe closer to fifty."

The agent withdrew his head from the window and waved the taxi through.

Nena's stomach unclenched and she breathed a sigh of relief.

"¿*Al Hotel Del Norte,* señorita?" the taxi driver inquired, regarding Nena in his rear view mirror. He hadn't spoken until then.

"Sí, por favor."

41

Nena felt a little silly walking into the venerable Del Norte with her bag of paper flowers and tourist stuff, but no one paid her any attention. The lobby was filled with noisy conventioneers enjoying free drinks, the ice in their glasses clanging, their conversations loud and raucous. She made her way through the crowd into the lounge, a cavernous, faux-marble hall that had once been the foyer. In the center of the room, high above the circular mahogany bar, the hotel's famous Tiffany glass dome glowed deep blue in the last of the day's light. In marked contrast to the tumultuous lobby, the place was quiet and nearly deserted.

Luis was nowhere in sight, nor did Nena see her uncle or the deputy. She settled into a high, wing-backed chair in a corner and set her market bag down beside her. A barmaid appeared and took her order for a Sprite. She picked up a tattered copy of *Texas Monthly* from the table in front of her and began absently leafing through it as she sipped her soft drink. She was half-heartedly reading a story about river-running on the Brazos when a familiar voice interrupted.

"Hola, Nena."

She looked up from the magazine. "Oh, my God. Ruben! Where's Luis?"

"I asked him to let me come for you. I can help you with this thing, Nena, if you'll let me."

A broad, shy smile lit up the detective's tan face as he stood peering down at her, his wide shoulders straining the seams of his Western-cut black tweed sport coat as he nervously shifted his weight from one shiny-booted foot to the other. Nena recognized the silver and turquoise bolo tie around his neck. She gave it to him one Christmas.

She put down the magazine and held Ruben in her gaze for a long moment before reaching her arms up to him. He took her hands and effortlessly pulled her to her feet. She collapsed against his chest, tears spilling onto his coat. "Oh, Ruben. I am so thankful you're here. You can't imagine what I've been through."

"I know all about it, Coyota. Luis told me everything. I was at the poker game with him last night when your uncle called. You don't have to talk about it now." Ruben's voice was like liquid chocolate, dark, warm, and smooth.

For several minutes neither spoke as they held each other. Nena broke the silence. She leaned back, held him at arm's length, and squinted up at him. "Do you ever drive an old APD blue and white?" she asked with a wry smile.

Ruben grinned like a kid with his hand caught in a cookie jar. "Oh, once in a while. In fact, that's what's parked outside. That retired workhorse is going to take us home."

"I should have known it was you escorting me home that night. You've been stalking me!"

Ruben laughed. "I have great news for you. A customs officer, Clark Bisbee, has come forward about those two men you heard talking at the airport, and an investigation is already underway. They might have killed your student because he was starting to spill the beans about DEA agents taking payoffs from drug pilots. And as for that garbage about you being a drug smuggler—I think those guys were trying to use trumped-up accusations to discredit you and scare you off."

"Me—a drug smuggler? Where did they get that?" She searched Ruben's large brown eyes, as if looking for an answer in them.

"Beats me. My source says that's the excuse they gave for following you down into Mexico."

Nena grew pensive. "I have another question."

"Uh huh."

"Am I ever going to be okay again? I mean, how am I going to get through this? I killed two people!"

"You're going to be fine, Nena. You can count on all of us to help you. You're a strong, courageous woman. A survivor. A true Coyota."

"Grandmother Libertad always told me to be like the coyotes, and I didn't forget. Ay, Ruben, it was such a horrible experience. I've never been so terrified in all my life. Hold me, guy, hold me."

"I've got you, Coyota. And this time I'm not letting you go."

*　　*　　*　　*　　*

ACKNOWLEDGMENTS

I'd like to thank my Brownie Troop leader, my 7th grade basketball coach, my screenwriter, my producers, my wardrobe mistress, my hair stylist—oh, wait! That's my Oscar speech. I'm getting ahead of myself.

I wouldn't even have gotten to the starting gate with *Coyota* if it weren't for a vicious, ruthless, venom-spitting, Red-Pen-of-Death wielding, slash-and-burn editor, who is usually disguised as mild-mannered, cat-cuddling, shy, and retiring Carol Eastes. Don't be fooled by appearances! One of those cats is a cat-o-nine-tails which she didn't hesitate to use on me the many, many times I tried to weasel out of working harder to make this manuscript the best it could be.

Nevertheless, any omissions, deletions, klunky phrases, repetitious repetitions, and other errata are all her fault, not mine. So there!

Many others contributed to this book with talent and gusto: Barbara Jellow, book designer; Cinny Green, copy editor; and Lauren Snyder, publicist; Frank Parrish, cover photograph; Elizabeth Cuéllar and Clark Lovell, Mexican locations; Prof. Rubén Cobos, the coyota definition; Ira Rimson, planes & guns. In myriad ways: Pili Arango, Brian Christian, Patrick Egan, Rosario Fiallos, Susan Frost, Gloria Giffords, Lynn Goldstein, Bennett Hammer, Ferdinand Joesten, the Pachamamas—Lolly Martin, Donna Herring, Mary Berkeley, and Spud; Deborah

Peacock, Jeff Radford, Gail Rieke, and Everybody I've Neglected To Name.

And of course, Frank Aon.

Many, many thanks.